I0648089

Still *Worlds* Collide:

PHILIP WYLIE

And the End of the American Dream

Clifford P. Bendau

BORGO PRESS / WILDSIDE PRESS

www.wildsidepress.com

For my wife Marlo,
who continues to understand

Library of Congress Cataloging in Publication Data:

Bendau, Clifford P   1950-
    Still worlds collide.

    (The Milford series: Popular writers of today ; v. 30) (ISSN 0163-2469)
    Bibliography: p. 62-63.
    1. Wylie, Philip, 1902-1971—Criticism and interpretation. I. Title.
PS3545.Y46Z57   813'.52   80-10756
ISBN 0-89370-144-0
ISBN 0-89370-244-7   OCLC #6016489

Copyright © 1980 by Clifford P. Bendau.
All rights reserved. No part of this book may be reproduced in any form without
the expressed written consent of the publisher. Published by arrangement with
the author. Printed in the United States of America by Victory, Press, San
Bernardino, California. Binding by California Zip Bindery, San Bernardino,
California.

Produced, designed, and published by R. Reginald, The Borgo Press, P.O. Box
2845, San Bernardino, CA 92406, USA. Composition by Irene Frost. Cover
design by Judy Cloyd Graphic Design.

First Edition———August, 1980

CHAPTER I:
Philip Wylie—The Reappearance

No less than Superman himself, the creator of the original Superman, Philip Wylie, burst forth from the unassuming facade of mild-mannered writer to become the "superwriter" of the Forties and Fifties. Representing truth, justice, and the American way, he was the voice of America and the vociferous critic of Americana. From his earliest novels through his polemical essays to his final work, he vehemently disapproved of his generation's decline in manners and morals. Out of his fiction and nonfiction alike came a portentous warning: awaken to the follies of the modern age or prepare to meet destruction and chaos in the future.

Tall and lanky, often appearing gaunt and drawn, Philip Wylie was an unimpressive figure to behold. He resembled neither athlete nor scholar. He was genteel and soft spoken, not likely to stand out in a crowd. But his books were boldly written and controversial, and he, as writer, was dashing and involved, a vital part of American life and letters. Curiously enough, Philip Wylie remains one of the least understood of twentieth-century American writers. He spoke the truth as he saw it, pointing out the hypocrisy and self-destructive patterns around him, revealing many aspects of America that Americans preferred not to know or think about. While lashing out at society, he remained perfectly cognizant of his own part in it, and fully believed that he would be equally responsible for its destruction if he did not act. So he did, by churning out hundreds of magazine articles, science fiction, adventure, romance, and mystery stories. But he was more than the proverbial ivory tower writer. He was also aggressively involved in anti-fascist activities in the Forties, with the Federal Civil Defense Administration in the Fifties, and was intimately connected with the Atomic Energy Commission and Lerner Research Laboratories in the Sixties. Throughout all, however, this sensitive writer was able to sustain his role as social critic without obscuring the poet within.

I know of no other author for whom writing came so easily as it did to Philip Wylie. In a career spanning fifty years, he produced about fifty books in hardcover, an equal number of serialized novels, and hundreds of short stories, articles, and essays, words at a phenomenal rate. One eighty-thousand word novel was written in eight days during a pleasure cruise. A shorter book was written in one day. When Wylie died on October 25, 1971, he had literally written himself to death.

Although Wylie's image declined in his later years, a change in the public's interest has recently become apparent. Wylie's place in American literature is again being discussed, articles are being written about him, his books are being reprinted. This reappearance is most welcome. My book examines Philip Wylie's contributions in the areas of fiction and nonfiction. It does not cover all of Wylie's work, but will focus upon the major writings in each of his developmental periods, first by introducing the reader to Philip Wylie and his work, second by discussing Wylie's historical development as a writer as revealed through a chronological survey and critical analysis of his books, with representative responses from the critical community.

The structure of this book reflects Wylie's own parabola of success. His early achievements in the Twenties and Thirties were in many ways the fore-runners to the monumental success of *Generation of Vipers* in 1943. It was in *Generation of Vipers* and four years later in *An Essay on Morals* that the germinal philosophical ideas found in the early fiction appeared in more didactic form. These explicitly stated ideas about Jung, instinct, and human values became the hub around which Wylie's fiction continued to evolve until 1968 when he wrote *The Magic Animal*. The themes, concerns, and principles of these three books comprise Wylie's "theory." All three are, therefore, treated in the section entitled "Theoretical Foundations." This short break in the chronological development is followed by further analyses of fiction, which relate these theoretical foundations to the writings of the Fifties, Sixties, and Seventies. In this way I have tried to avoid isolating individual works, instead interrelating Wylie's life, theory, and fiction.

It would clearly be misleading to suggest that this critique could convey all that is necessary for an understanding of Wylie's canon. For those who desire further coverage and analysis, I recommend Truman F. Keefer's *Philip Wylie* and the chapter in Sam Moskowitz's *Explorers of the Infinite* entitled "Space Opus: Philip Wylie." Both are excellent studies that may provide the reader with other points of view.

Biographical Background

Wylie's life has been well documented in Truman F. Keefer's *Philip Wylie*, Sam Moskowitz's *Explorers of the Infinite*, and H. R. Warfel's *American Novelists of Today*. Philip Gordon Wylie was born in Beverly, Massachusetts, on May 12, 1902. His father was a moderately successful Presbyterian minister, whose love of the outdoors and disdain for religion were both transmitted to his son. His mother, a fiction writer, died when Philip was five. Both parents were descended from Scottish families that had migrated to America in the seventeenth and eighteenth centuries. With bloodlines going back to Jonathan Edwards, Philip was "a product of and rebel against the last great Puritan establishment" (PW, p.18). His siblings included Max Wylie, also destined to become a writer, Verona, and half-brother Edward.

Wylie's earliest years are interesting and informative. Edna Edwards Wylie's early death had far-reaching consequences on her son. Keefer, who studies the relationship between Wylie's life experiences and maturation as a writer, concludes that Philip was scarred by this early loss and would be forever bothered by the apparent tenuousness of life. Philip, Keefer points out, would write "with a smoldering rage against the pain and meaninglessness" of this early suffering. Characterization in future novels would reveal the warm memory of his angelic mother and the painful image of his hypocritical father.

Philip's interest in science and the scientific method developed early and became a cornerstone of his mature writing. Moskowitz points out that Philip was an avid reader of Jules Verne and H. G. Wells, and had "practically memorized the children's *Book of Knowledge* by the time he was twelve" (EoI, p.281). But it was during his college years at Princeton that, forced to study the hard sciences, evolutionary biology, and psychology, he was exposed to Darwin, Freud, and Jung, all of whom became major influences in his thinking; it was the scientific method itself that linked these influences together.

Though Wylie claimed to have published his first piece at twelve, he began his serious writing while at Princeton. Wylie's sophisticated satires and parodies of nineteenth century authors appeared in the *Princetonian* under several pseudonyms. This writing, though appreciated by fellow classmates, was not taken seriously by university savants, with one claiming that the sardonic student would "never even write a label for a soupcan!" (PW, p.32). It is therefore not surprising that Wylie, after a conflict with a literature professor over a final exam, departed from Princeton without a degree. This disenchantment with education and educators would mark his later writing.

Leaving Princeton, Wylie attempted a career in advertising and public relations, eventually becoming a staff writer for *New Yorker* magazine. Here he was involved in everything from layout and design to writing unsigned entries for "The Talk of the Town." In 1927, after being dropped from the magazine staff, he was forced into freelance work. From this point on, he earned his income entirely through writing.

Philosophical Overview

Wylie became one of the most ambitious and outspoken writers of the twentieth century. Although he was not a product of the university, he felt comfortable with its most sophisticated concepts, considering his self-acquired knowledge equivalent to several doctorates. His irreverence for academic propriety was legend, as was his prolificacy. He was a generalist who scoffed at those specialists who were unable to follow a problem from start to finish, and he took great pleasure in flouting scholarly "rules."

5

He was primarily concerned with truth. He believed mankind to be suffering from chronic self-deception. He saw humanity taking refuge in falsehood whenever life became too difficult. By inveighing wrathfully against self-imposed blindness, he made himself the gadfly to the mid-twentieth-century Americans. With books that attempted to "throw light on the curtain we Americans draw across our minds," his mission was to reveal "the gulf between our pretensions and what we really do."

No single area could have contained Philip Wylie's bursting energy. He jumped into controversy. He studied human nature, searching for and formulating new theories about man's tendency to self-destruction. It was a lifetime endeavor. His half-century of writing was a search for order. Using the intellectual evangelism he inherited from his father, he mercilessly exposed the sin of self-deception. With missionary zeal, Wylie sought to convert those who believed in disordered superstition into science-minded believers.

Science was his first love: it met the need for honest investigation. Wylie's universe was orderly and rational; it could be investigated by the scientific method. Although science meant different things at different times to him, rational thinking characterized his writing. His early books would employ the hard physical sciences. His fiction, especially his science fiction, would prove that a writer could be scientifically accurate *and* interesting. Using a contemporary understanding of physics, chemistry, biology, and mathematics, Wylie projected future technologies, always balancing scientific realism with inventiveness. This is most evident in his early speculative fantasies.

The soft sciences marked Wylie's middle years. Psychology (not the behavioristic variety of Watson or Dewey, but the depth-psychology of Freud and Jung) became the hub of his writing. Wylie reasoned that man was an animal with animal instincts. To deny this because of egoistic-religious reasons was the cause of modern man's apparent insanity. Drawing first on Freud and then on Jung, Wylie argued that instinct was of prime importance in man. Man could not deny the existence of instinct without producing dire consequences. These ideas are clearly presented in Wylie's nonfiction such as *Generation of Vipers* and *An Essay on Morals* and in novels such as *Opus 21* and *The Disappearance*.

In his final years, science included the biological sciences and the conclusions of naturalists. The natural sciences, dealing with man's evolutionary nature, reaffirmed Wylie's belief in man's animal instincts. He would take issue with those who denied man's animal nature, drawing on men like Konrad Lorenz and Robert Ardrey, and then arguing through analogy. This phase of Wylie's thought is definitively written in *The Magic Animal* (1968) and the posthumously published novel, *The End of the Dream* (1971).

Although his career is neatly delineated into different scientific orientations, the various objects of Wylie's hostility give the best clue to his major concerns: man's destruction of man, dogmatic thinking, the destruction of the environment, and the relationship between the sexes.

History takes strange and irregular courses, but always seems to repeat itself. Wylie, a household word in the Forties and Fifties, was pushed aside in the social upheaval of the Sixties and Seventies. Competing with radical polemicists and voices for radical social change, Wylie, although an earlier force for change himself, could not pierce the veil of the generation gap. The spokesman for the "new morality" in the Thirties was now considered a representative of the old morality. By the time of his death, Wylie was once again an obscure writer known primarily in science fiction circles. Even today he is remembered primarily as the prolific iconoclast who added the word "momism" to the American lexicon, or he is described as a writer of overstated and splenetic books and magazine articles.

And now there is a new interest in Philip Wylie. A few of his books have been reprinted—others are certain to be. Yet, in spite of this new interest, it is no simple task to obtain information about Wylie. Many books remain out of print. Those in print are seldom found in bookstores and have disappeared from library shelves. Even the Philip Wylie manuscript collection in Princeton's Firestone Library is uncatalogued!

While Wylie's influence on modern literature may have been slight, the key to his importance lies in his visionary themes. Although the sheer quantity of Wylie's accumulated work is overwhelming, there are some constants which unify the whole. These constants, clearly delineated in Wylie's nonfiction, provide guidelines for his fiction, the arena where the theoretical basis of his philosophy was tested and challenged. Outside of his contributions to *Harper's*, *Saturday Evening Post*, and many other magazines and periodicals, his definitive nonfiction statement was *Generation of Vipers*. Four years later he wrote another, *An Essay on Morals*, to clarify and expand upon some of the points made in *Vipers*. Between the two came a massive outpouring of essays and articles reiterating his positions and clarifying his ideas. In 1968, after discovering the ideas of several naturalists, he wrote *The Magic Animal*, the definitive nonfiction statement of his later years. Here, the reader will find new positions and ideas, some contradictory and others adding to his early beliefs about man's nature. Finally, in the last year of his life, 1971, Wylie completed a final nonfiction book entitled *The Sons and Daughters of Mom*, taking umbrage with the problems of the late Sixties and early Seventies.

Clearly his canon is heavily weighed on the side of fiction. It is reasonable to conclude that the nonfiction and fiction are both spinoffs of similar principles and concerns. In an attempt to choose novels that are relevant to my discussions of Wylie's philosophical concerns, I have arbitrarily chosen certain works for more extensive analyses than others. *Gladiator*, reprinted by Hyperion Press in 1974, is particularly relevant today, as is *The Disappearance*, which was reprinted in 1978 by Warner Books, and remains one of Wylie's most socially relevant works. *When Worlds Collide* and *After Worlds Collide* have become science fiction classics, and although coauthored with Edwin Balmer, owe much more to Wylie's input than the public ever realized. These are covered in depth. The philosophical novels *Finnley Wren* and *Night Unto Night*, as well as the disaster novels *Tomorrow*, *Triumph*, and *The End of the Dream*, reflect certain aspects of Wylie's thought, and are given particular attention.

Philip Wylie was one of the most prophetic, persuasive, and currently relevant thinkers of the mid-twentieth century. Although revered by some and reviled by others, few can deny the validity of his concerns, the forthrightness of his conclusions, or the impact of his style. The complete honesty with which he confronted his times gave us an early glimpse of a world we are presently struggling with. America was never the same after *Generation of Vipers*, perhaps because Americans were finally exposed to themselves for what they were—human.

CHAPTER II:
The Early Achievements

There is no simple Philip Wylie. His work is developmental, rapidly evolving and changing, throughout his career. The years prior to the publication of *Generation of Vipers* (1942) were marked by moderate success, but were primarily an apprenticeship period. While Wylie's novels gained him a reputation as a promising writer, and his book sales reached acceptable levels, most of his income came from magazine publications. His ability to write acceptable prose rapidly made him a regular contributor to *Harper's*, *Saturday Evening Post*, and later *Redbook*. By the early Forties he was earning a five-figure annual income, but had not yet gained national fame.

Heavy Laden (1928)

Wylie's career began with publication of *Heavy Laden*, a "novel of manners" with strong autobiographical overtones. Written on assignment for Knopf (which had accepted but not published an earlier work), the book was an impressive first novel, focusing on the conflicts between father and daughter. The real subject, however, was Wylie's indictment of an entire generation's moral hypocrisy.

The story portrays the relationship of Presbyterian minister Hugh McGreggor with his daughter Ann. Like any novel of manners, there is a questioning of social values. McGreggor, a self-righteous and forceful man of God, fights the temptations of vice so passionately that he is blinded to the reality around him. Ann, "a young girl of the type that has succeeded the flapper," embodies the morality of the "new generation." Father and daughter are set against each other in what we now recognize as the "generation gap."

By portraying Hugh McGreggor as the moral sanitation director of small town America, a man who neither feels nor empathizes with anything but his own rectitude, and Ann as free-wheeling and materialistic, Wylie has grounded his story in irrepressible conflict. Whereas Hugh, a man of faith, grasps the mysticism of God's works and uncompromisingly crusades for moral earnestness, his daughter Ann is a woman of reason, who is intellectually independent and scientific-minded. Their conflict is the conflict of the new morality in a century of science: reason over faith.

Heavy Laden, like any first novel, has its flaws. Wylie's relationship with his own father, observes biographer Truman F. Keefer, is mirrored in the story. McGreggor, like the Reverend Edward Wylie, is closed-minded and vicious, yet courageous and strong. For both, there is a genuine incapacity to understand either their children or the general changes in society. The result is a tragic displacement. McGreggor's tragedy, writes Keefer, "is not just that he is an anachronism or even that he drives his children from him: rather, it is that he despoils his own potential and in the end becomes a hypocrite" (PW, p.31). This is what Wylie saw in his own father. Autobiographical tendencies do not always provide firm foundations for fiction, and fortunately they eventually faded out of Wylie's novels. His distaste for self-deception and hypocrisy remained, however, and grew stronger with each new book.

Critical response to *Heavy Laden* was encouraging. While one critic commented that Wylie "had the time of his life writing the book," another, Marjory Latimer of *The New York Times*, was surprised that "such a welter of impressionism, bombast, excellent writing, and sensationalism at all costs" could be contained within one book cover. Subject matter, grumbled some, was a little questionable: "It will disgust all those who have a definite notion of what is decent in a novel," exclaimed *Saturday Review*'s Robert MacDougall, though no one, he goes on, "can deny its occasional brilliance."

Heavy Laden was didactic and suffered from the author's poor choice of narrative technique. A writer who addresses the reader directly can be an obtrusive force, often a nuisance or distraction. Wylie's insertion of his own voice into the story was damaging but not fatal. Whether the young author was consciously borrowing from Fielding is uncertain, but there is no question that Fielding used the technique more effectively. Nevertheless, the novel worked, despite the minor flaws. Wylie's affinity for truth stood out, as did his irreverence for repressively Victorian morality. Because he touched on the unmentionable areas of sex and debauchery among young people, Wylie earned the reputation as spokesman for the "now" generation, and as advocate for a broadened new morality. This is not entirely true. Wylie, as the critics would soon learn, spoke only for himself and for his perception of truth, though irreverent nose-thumbing at others' perceptions of truth can be correctly identified with his early writing.

American values seemed to him to be grounded in self-deception and superficiality, and this enraged Wylie even at the earliest stages of his career. He disliked hypocrisy wherever he perceived it. Religion, the interaction between the sexes, and the phenomenon of big business were but a few of Wylie's targets. He would attack them directly later in his career, but in the earliest stages he relied on more thinly-sheathed fiction. Uncertain of the validity of conventional marriage, Wylie in his second novel experimented with unconventionality.

Babes and Sucklings (1929)

Babes and Sucklings (1929), which appeared less than one year after *Heavy Laden*, is a moral statement about life amidst changing values. Although similar in subject matter to the earlier book, it is more sensitively written and stylistically refined; there is also less invective. Wylie tones down his intellectual vocabulary and stops addressing his readers through the narrator. Both novels can be classified as novels of manners.

In *Babes* we meet Cynthia Sherman and a young man named Thorton. The story follows them through their joint experiences, charting their growth as they evolve and change through the contact with each other and the "modern world." Cynthia is a California girl who flees to New York in search of someone better than her soon-to-be ex-husband. At a party in New York she meets Thorton, an interesting man with a striking resemblance to the author. They fall in love and begin an unconventional relationship without the need for marriage. Most of this voyeuristic novel observes and analyzes the two lovers as they struggle with their relationship and own inner complexities. The plot is weak and meandering, but the characterization is strong.

Babes and Sucklings questions the established conventions of marriage: can two people, different in temperament, succeed in a relationship that is not sanctioned by marriage? Wylie's answer is yes, but not without qualifications. Cynthia and Thorton's happiness is threatened by a number of problems, including career frustration, miscarriage, and separation. In spite of these difficulties the two are ultimately reunited, and, in the end, marry.

Wylie's ability to create sensitive, living, and believable characters is apparent in this second novel. His characters are less "types" than in *Heavy Laden*. Each is unique and each has his or her own subtle motivations, inner complexity, and background. Keefer calls this book Wylie's most "convincing picture of human relationship," because the scenes "involve subtle changes of attitude or mood, small discoveries and decisions, moments of communication or alienation." Wylie is clearly growing more sensitive and observant, more knowledgeable about human emotions, and more restrained. He continues to attack the establishment, but now reveals a new weapon: charm.

Critics responded less favorably to *Babes and Sucklings* than to *Heavy Laden*. Wylie's literary "bad mannerism" had not improved, wrote one critic, but "he has at least reconciled his animosities to a consistent literary style." Another was exasperated because Wylie "succeeded in making vice as boring as virtue," and reiterated that the young author must have felt the need to get something off his chest "at the cost of jerky construction, banal plot, and prolonged preachments."

If the measure of success in fiction lies in characters revealing themselves through action, and plot proving character, then Wylie's second novel falls short. Thorton and Cynthia are sensitively drawn, but are enervated by the lack of dynamic action, at times appearing similar to daytime soap-opera characters. Although Wylie was a future polemicist in seed, his earliest characters had a problem with philosophizing. This would change with *Finnley Wren*, a true philosophical novel, but *Finnley* was five years in the future. Wylie's next published novel, *Gladiator*, turns instead toward the dramatization of a particular subject.

Gladiator; Blondy's Boy Friend (1930)

Wylie's third book, *Gladiator*, represents a change in direction. More akin to a fable than a fully developed novel, this deceptively simple rewrite of an earlier work was, according to some, the prototype for the comic strip hero Superman. Sam Moskowitz points out that the creators of Superman not only "borrowed the central theme of *Gladiator*," but actually paraphrased some of the dialogue.

Wylie attempts to free his readers' imagination with a metaphor, a traditional fable-like beginning: "Once upon a time in Colorado lived a man named Abednego Danner and his wife, Matilda." Danner is a "spindling wisp of a man" who teaches biology at the local college; his wife is a woman "who understood nothing and undertook all." Mild-mannered Abednego develops a serum which alters the molecular structure of a developing fetus. His experiments produce tadpoles capable of swimming through plate glass and a cat that can crash through walls and eat cows. Abednego secretly injects his pregnant wife, who, nine months later, gives birth to Hugo, a child who smashes his crib, holds himself above his babychair with one hand, and hurtles out of second-storey windows. The secret, obviously, is short-lived.

Hugo can lift several tons over his head, jump fifty feet in the air, run with blinding speed, and build fortresses out of heavy boulders. He is invulnerable to physical injury, but has the emotional vulnerability of a normal boy. Unable to reveal his superpowers, he is forced to live in a solitary world, one marked by loneliness and isolation. The story follows Hugo as he begins life's journey, experiencing the pettiness of his fellow men, and finally succumbing to total disillusionment and despair.

Hugo, a star athlete in college, unwittingly kills an opponent on the football field. His flight from guilt takes him to the South Seas, to carnival freak shows, and eventually to war. Throughout all of his experiences his extraordinary powers bring pain and suffering. His life is marked by disaster, death, and futility. His desire to use his super powers for good purposes is continually thwarted by ordinary people who fear, envy, and use him. From beginning to end, his life is a series of physical and spiritual disasters.

Hugo meets an archaeologist, a man of reason, who suggests that Hugo retrieve Abednego's formula and create a race of Titans; Danner at first agrees, hoping to save mankind. When he realizes, however, just how human this super race would be, he rejects the offer. Hugo Danner, frustrated and angry, seeing no hope for either mankind or himself, prays to be destroyed and is mercifully struck down by a lightning bolt. Nothing in life can provide Hugo Danner with the understanding or compassion that he needs. Despite his powers, he dies alone on a hill, a superior man without a place in the world of ordinary people.

Gladiator is a simple tale, but reveals much about young Philip Wylie. He would often write about the plight of the "truly superior person." Wylie saw, as others did before him, that the mediocre are happy being mediocre. Several critics speak of the "serious theme" at work here. Keefer writes that it was Wylie's belief that ". . .when a truly superior person tries to win acceptance and puts his talents to use in the world, he will be frustrated and defeated by mankind's stupidity, pettiness, jealousy, unenlightened self-interest, and indifference to moral principles" (PW, p.46). Other critics were more mystified. While the novel was innovative, the idea itself was criticized for being "too good." The premises were so fantastic, some critics concluded, that "there could be no logical conclusion;" the story, they felt, could not be "properly finished." Some felt that *Gladiator* showed no development over earlier novels and that the author, "obviously talented, lacked literary common sense." Actually, Wylie did create an interesting premise, so good that it ultimately was warped and stolen.

Carelessly read, *Gladiator* might seem like the ego projection of another Walter Mitty. Actually, this is a story full of conflict, and from a strictly literary point of view, the novel stands on its own. The theme is almost Nietzschean. The truly superior person cannot be accepted by the *hoi polloi*. The masses, unable to see beyond their herd mentality, are quick to destroy all that is not as mediocre as themselves. The superior man must stand alone. All of these ideas permeate the tragedy of Hugo Danner, whose tragic flaw is, perhaps, the presence of very normal emotions within his extraordinary body. Life is just too painful for Hugo Danner or for any giving and emotional person who will, reasons Wylie, be sucked under by self-serving charlatans and unfeeling hypocrites. This is the theme communicated through the often-contrived action scenes, as well as in Hugo's solitary moments of despair. In each incident, it is the simplicity of Wylie's expression that communicates with the most impact.

Although *Gladiator* lacks the subtlety of *Babes and Sucklings*, with a plot that is ultimately unrealistic, the novel's allegorical structure is the blueprint for many of Wylie's future stories and novels. The story is blunt and moralistic by today's standards, but considered within the framework of its own time, is conceptually sound and lends itself to the author's purpose.

Unfortunately, this is not true for *Blondy's Boy Friend*, also published in 1930 under the pseudonym Leatrice Homesley. Truman Keefer, the first critic to include *Blondy* in Wylie's canon, comments that this sickly work is a good example of Wylie's early inability to write popular fiction. The story is amateurishly conceived, and a good example of Wylie at his worst.

Wylie often borrowed from other sources. While his early novels display a fascination for collective myths and legends, his later works employ literary allusion more effectively. Symbolism, virtually absent in these early writings, will become an important element of Wylie's later work.

The Murderer Invisible; Footprints of Cinderella (1931)

The Murderer Invisible draws heavily from H. G. Wells's famous story, *The Invisible Man*. Once again enticing the reader through fantasy while sustaining a serious theme, Wylie gives his protagonist the ability to become invisible at will. Like *Gladiator*, *Murderer* incorporates the logic of science within a truly superior individual; and although each book utilizes differently-motivated character types, they actually deal with the same theme. Hugo Danner took his secret to the grave, because he knew what ordinary men would do with it. *The Murderer Invisible* confirms the wisdom of not creating a race of Titans "by showing what happens when another superman, the possessor of the greatest scientific brain in the world, elects, instead, to use whatever force is necessary to impose his vision of utopia on his fellow man'' (PW, p.54). Unfortunately, the story is not as well written, the action being unimaginative and the movement slow.

Although Wylie makes no claims for originality, the influence of Wells's book jumps out at the reader. Both novels, in fact, use the "identical method of achieving invisiblity, attaining the ultimate transparency of all bone and body tissue after neutralizing all color and pigment" (EoI, p.282). Ironically, although Wells's novel was the prototype for Wylie's story, Universal Studios purchased the movie rights to both versions, when they decided to produce their film, *The Invisible Man*, and incorporated elements of both into their final product (EoI, p.282).

Wylie's next novel was a modern version of the Cinderella fable. Originally written for *Redbook* and then published in book form in 1931, *Footprints of Cinderella* is best described as light romantic fiction, another poorly-written soap opera. The motivations of the characters are seldom revealed, there is an absence of description, and the people are stark, even boring.

Jealous Aunt Chloe switches her brother's daughter at birth with a French child, but is thwarted in her evil scheme before it pays off. The wealthy brother's inheritance is withheld until proper identification of his daughter is made. The rest of the story is simply a search for and proof of the real Cinderella.

While the traditional Cinderella fairy tale is "a light-hearted story," comments Keefer in his analysis, "Wylie's insertion of weighty matters on momism and Freudian aberrations requires a thoughtful approach to all events that occur" (PW, p.61). Thought is anathema to light popular fiction, and Wylie loads this story down with discussion and debate. Most readers were disappointed—most critics panned the book. Wylie's Cinderella story was soon forgotten, but would, in different form, emerge again in the Forties.

When Worlds Collide (1932); After Worlds Collide (1934)

During the early Thirties, Wylie, still a fledgling writer, began a working relationship with Edwin Balmer, the editor of *Redbook*, collaborating with him on several serialized and book-length novels, including the murder mysteries *Five Fatal Words* (1931), *The Golden Hoard* (1933), and *The Shield of Silence* (1935). Their most fortunate collaboration, the two-part novel *When Worlds Collide* and *After Worlds Collide*, quickly became a science fiction classic.

In science fiction, as in literature in general, collaborative writing is the exception rather than the rule. Many collaborations come about less for artistic reasons than for purposes of expediency—this was certainly the case with Wylie and Balmer. Balmer's strong point was his ability to construct strong, suspenseful plots—he was not a literary craftsman. Wylie was able to inject a certain measure of scientific realism into his work, and could produce on demand. His weakness, more of inexperience than lack of ability, was in organizing a tightly-structured story line. The alliance between these two men of complementary talents proved to be profitable, not only to the writers themselves, but also to the future of science fiction literature.

When Worlds Collide was the principal success of the Balmer-Wylie team. Originally titled *These Shall not Die*, it was first published in 1932 as a magazine serial, then reissued in book form in 1933. The novel has proved to be one of the most popular science fiction stories ever written, very quickly becoming a classic in the field. Released in a year that was already experiencing the economic end of the world, this story of the physical end of the world, focusing on scientific realism rather than pure adventure, was well received. Man's ability to overcome adversity through human enterprise and science would be a recurring theme in future science fiction.

The use of cosmic catastrophe as the motivating force in a novel is not unusual. The archetypal dread of world's end can be found in man's earliest writings, reflecting one of the most basic of human fears. *When Worlds Collide* builds on this baleful possibility, documenting what takes place on Earth after the scientific discovery that the world is going to end. While the outline and plot have been attributed to Edwin Balmer, the action itself, teeming with lurid descriptions of natural disaster and the depravity of humanity's masses, is clearly Philip Wylie's.

The utilization of an "end of the world" theme enabled the authors to incorporate visionary technologies and allegorical imagery into their presentation of conventional science fiction and stock romantic themes. Set in the United States midway through the twentieth century, the action-packed story moves rapidly from one incident to another. The most visible flaw is incomplete situational development, undoubtedly the result of the magazine serialization.

The characterization in *When Worlds Collide* is similar to other Wylie novels. The heroes are brave, level-headed, scientific-minded individuals who are able to rise above the less-than-rational mass of humanity. Tony Drake, the prime mover in the story, is an athletic, well-bred New York stockbroker who is intelligent and "entirely normal." His romantic counterpart, another typical Wylie character, is Eve Hendron. A daughter of Dr. Cole Hendron, the renowned American astrophysicist and engineer, Eve is remarkably intelligent and beautiful "in her own right." In fact, she is from the beginning one of the few capable of dealing rationally with the impending disaster. It is only because Tony is present at the Hendron residence when a courier arrives that he is peripherally informed about the frightening possibilities of the future. Dave Ransdell, war hero and flier from South Africa, is introduced into the story as he delivers top secret photographic plates from an observatory in South Africa to Dr. Hendron. Sent by Lord Rhondin, the Governor of the South African Dominion, the plates confirm a South African astronomer's discovery of two celestial bodies hurtling through space toward Earth. Sven Bronson's calculations show that a large body, Bronson Alpha, and its smaller satellite, Bronson Beta, will pass once, circle the sun, and return to destroy the world. This momentary meeting between Ransdell, Drake, and the Hendrons portends the future. The reader is given not only a glimpse of the apocalyptic developments to come, but also an introduction to the romantic triangle which is seemingly included to provide intermittent relief from the carefully-plotted dramatic tension. The recurring romantic interludes are superfluous, weak in characterization, trite in substance, and unbelievable in dialogue.

In most doomsday stories there appears some glimmer of hope—a way out. It is no different here. While the larger Bronson Alpha will most certainly collide with and destroy the Earth, the smaller Bronson Beta will continue on its course and begin orbiting the solar system. This planet, if inhabitable, is the only hope. The League of the Last Days, a select group of scientists under the direction of Dr. Hendron, has already begun the monumental task of constructing a vessel capable of transporting a small group of pilgrims to Bronson Beta.

One weakness of the book is Wylie's continual use of biblical allegory. The fire-and-brimstone quality of the story, characteristic of the minister's son, is often hard to take, and the discussions about the future tend to be mildly evangelistic. The story is ripe with religious fervor. Direct quotes and indirect allusions to the Bible are frequent: the finger of God is pointing to Earth; the world is to be destroyed, cleansed of its sin; Bronson Beta is the second chance, the softening of God's anger. The spaceship under construction is likened to Noah's vessel—in fact, actually named the *Ark*. The "morally upright," which for Wylie is often synonymous with "those trained in the sciences," are saved and allowed to reestablish sane laws and old morality. The story is weakened at key points by Wylie's adulation of intellectuals and deprecation of the bovine masses. The outcome of many situations is predictable to anyone familiar with the Cowboy-and-Indian genre. Nevertheless, Wylie's visionary accounts of atomic power used for destructive purposes, the accuracy of his scientific discussions, and his fastidiously detailed discussions of space travel overrule the occasional heavy-handed appeals to heaven and justice.

Misanthropic accounts of societal disintegration are characteristic of Wylie's almost gruesome fascination with the baseness at the heart of humanity. Predictably, the masses refuse to believe what is undeniable. Even as the celestial bodies approach the gravitational field of the Earth and *terra firma* becomes a seething hell, the great hoards of mankind revert to primitive savagery. The first passage of the Bronson bodies brings forth unimaginable destruction. The description of terrestrial disaster is terrifying: lower elevations on the coastlines are inundated by floodwaters; volcanic eruptions belch out death and destruction; hurricane-force winds fling buildings like paper; cataclysmic earthquakes swallow entire continents. Hell is opening its jaws and ingesting the sinners. One half of Earth's population is gone. Even the Moon, caught in the path of Bronson Alpha, is snuffed out with metaphorical significance.

The Hendron group, confined to one large camp in Michigan, survives the first passage. After an exploration team accidentally discovers a metal which proves capable of withstanding the stresses of the upcoming flight, the *Ark* is completed. The discovery of the all-important metal, another indication of God's benevolent intervention, enables the group to construct a second ship. All will be saved. Unfortunately, the violence in the heavens is matched by man-made violence on Earth. The bloodthirsty survivors of the first passing attack Hendron's camp, killing many of the pilgrims. Nonetheless, on the predicted day of collision, the two ships depart for Bronson Beta. The Earth is destroyed. Whether or not any other ships escape is not known or revealed.

After Worlds Collide continues the characterization and underlying issues of the previous book. It follows the space pilgrims through the process of rebirth on Bronson Beta. Beginning with the successful landing on the new planet, the action follows Dr. Cole Hendron, now an aging Moses-like figure; Tony Drake, who is handed the reins of power; David Ransdell, who remains the brave explorer; and Eve, who shows little, if any growth. The story records the birth pangs of the new society, chronicles the discovery of the magnificent remains of a mysterious civilization that had vanished from Bronson Beta centuries earlier, and details the conflict with another group of settlers who have also escaped the Earth's destruction.

The sequel is inferior to the original. While there is ingenious description of futuristic advancements achieved by the previous inhabitants of Bronson Beta, much of the book focuses on the conflict between the American settlers and their Asiatic counterparts. There is a xenophobic quality to the battling between the "good" Americans and the "evil" Asiatics, much of it attributable to the era in which the story was written. In general, the characters remain static, and although there are a few surprising revelations which are contrived for the development of plot, there is little growth present. Perhaps the most tantalizing issue in the story, one that permeates it throughout, is the question of what happened to the previous inhabitants, all of whom have disappeared without a trace. Most of the story prods the reader with this question, and though an answer of sorts is proposed, the story is never satisfactorily concluded.

The Bronson Beta books are classic "good guys versus bad guys" stories, with the bad guys being society's uninformed masses, and the good guys the science-minded intellectuals. The authors' violent, evangelistic message states that only those who pursue the vision of science will ultimately be saved. The duo was to be followed with a sequel which would explain the secret of the missing inhabitants of Bronson Beta. Although actually outlined by Balmer, the projected book was vetoed by Wylie. Wylie, a fastidious adherent to scientific detail and accuracy, refused to collaborate on a story which could not be validated. The two original successes were combined into one volume by the Lippincott Publishing Company in 1950, filmed by Paramount in 1951, and remain in print even today, after most of Wylie's work has long been forgotten.

The Savage Gentleman (1932)

Wylie's growing disdain for American morals and, more precisely, the attitudes of American women, is revealed in *The Savage Gentleman*. This Robinsonade develops a situation that, although unlikely, is less fantastic than either *Gladiator* or *The Murderer Invisible*. Stephen Stone, a wealthy newspaperman who is disenchanted with his marriage, gathers his son and two helpers, departs on his yacht, and deliberately runs aground on an obscure island. Stranded on the unknown isle, away from the perverted elements of civilization, Stone, a Negro servant, and an engineer friend attempt to educate young Henry Stone. After thirty years of isolated edu-

16

cation and rearing, Henry's father dies and leaves him his fortune; and the other men are rescued and transported to New York. Henry, innocent to the decadence of civilization, runs into problems with corruption and graft. His contacts with unscrupulous women, coupled with his lack of sophistication, combine to create an extremely problematic situation. His natural virtue and moral earnestness eventually surface, but not before he has singlehandedly beat up half of the city of New York while in a fit of rage. The ending is upbeat, with Henry deciding to use his influence via the newspaper to fight for the forces of good. Even the male-female battle is quelled when Henry relaxes his strict sexual and emotional standards.

Throughout his early work, Wylie communicated emotion caustically, his characters often manhandling the movement or direction of the story through angry diatribe, although their very frustration with life or their particular situation inevitably created dramatic action. *The Savage Gentleman* does not reveal any pattern of related feelings in its characters, but peppers the reader with the blunt emotions of anger and frustration. Once again, Wylie is too close to the action: in this book, his opinions, always strong, repeatedly come between his characters and his readers—his beliefs are expressed at the expense of the action.

One critic notes the contrived story line, but points out that "this romantic tale soon captures one's interest and steadily tightens its grip as the well-wrought and ingenious action progresses to a close." Another critic, mentioning the "dull and uninteresting" character, agrees that the "ingenious plot" provides "excitement in plenty." Yet in the end I agree with Keefer, who believes that Wylie was unable to come up with anything "original, enlightening, or even entertaining for his hero to do." The book is sententious, though it begins to reveal an attitude about women that would ripen and stir controversy ten years later in *Generation of Vipers*. Sam Moskowitz distilled the most characteristic passage from the book. In a line delivered by Stephen Stone to his son Henry, the elder Stone states: "Never, never, never believe a woman. . .women are ruin. Love is a myth. Marry when you are over forty-five and marry someone you do not love. Love is ruin" (EoI, p.284). Wylie continued to deliver seething diatribes against women for another decade. Then, after the release of *Generation of Vipers*, he became the "man who hated women."

Representative Articles and Films (1930-1935)

Wylie, by 1932, was a promising writer. Critics knew him as shockingly modern, pugnacious, dauntless. His books challenged the establishment, most often approaching subject matter best left alone. While his novels reached acceptable sales levels, he was best known at this time for his magazine writing, which earned him most of his income. Popular magazines, often "pulp" magazines, were Wylie's soapboxes. His stories and essays in these publications give a clear picture of the man and his thinking, and even at this early time, give hints of what was to come.

"Why Colleges Fail Students," appearing in *Saturday Evening Post* in December, 1930, was an outspoken attack on anachronistic attitudes and practices within the American system of higher education. Wylie, who had never graduated from Princeton, believed that established college curricula and narrow-visioned pedants were ruining young minds. The smart ones, he reasons, fled the university before it was too late. The others flunked out. In either case it was the college that was failing students, not students failing college. Drawing upon his own experiences of eight years earlier (though not stating that directly) Wylie's indictment places the blame on inadequate curricula that did not provide the student with an opportunity to think, stressed courses in dead languages, and reduced modern English to vocabulary and grammar alone, making literature as exciting as memorizing a phone book. No, concludes Wylie, there is nothing wrong with American youth. They are smart enough to reject the mass of pap they are fed. After all, he snipes, Booth Tarkington and Eugene O'Neill each attended Princeton for a few years, dropped out, and went on to become successful writers. And, the implication goes, so will Philip Wylie.

Another early attempt to expose irrationality in American institutions and attitudes was "The Quitter as Hero." Appearing in the October, 1930, issue of *Harper's Magazine*, this short piece defied the American "stick-to-itiveness" attitude. Wylie, in apparent justification of his own abandonment of Princeton, advised that "excepting an adherence to one's self and generally to one's country" there is "nothing else upon the horizon of human activity to which it is essential that one must cling forever." What is quintessential, he goes on, is the ability to "give up an idea and accept a new one." This "liquidity" is essential to progress, the most characteristic element of the scientific attitude. The recognition of error, the admission of guilt, and the attempt to reconstruct all, though central to Wylie's thoughts at this early point in his career, would reappear ten years later in *Generation of Vipers*.

Two other articles were wholly characteristic of Wylie's early years. "The Russians Have Beards," published in *Saturday Evening Post* in 1931, sarcastically questions the then-present reverence for the "Reds," and satirically concludes that it is because the "Russians have beards." Attacking the American "pink-eyed intelligentsia," Wylie taunts the liberal-intellectuals because they are intimidated by the bearded visages of the most boring nationality in the world. "It is time for Americans," concludes Wylie, "to yawn in the Russians' faces." This early anti-Russian article began a lifetime of attacks on the Soviets, whom Wylie would later accuse of murdering his half-brother while the two men were visiting the Soviet Union.

Wylie's earliest tirades against hypocrisy in America would, throughout the years, gather density like a snowball plummeting down a hillside. As he matured he felt less compelled to justify his own actions, but he would always be concerned with those issues that touched him personally. A lighter, but no less personal article appeared in the November, 1933, issue of *Harper's*. "How to Write for the Movies" is a painfully long and drawn out explication of the process of scriptwriting. The article itself is dull, but does bring out another aspect of Wylie's versatility.

Screenplay writing played a large role in Wylie's life during the Thirties. His screenplay credits include three films for Paramount: the 1932 classic,

Island of Lost Souls, which was written with Waldemar Young, *Murder in the Zoo* (1933), which starred Lionel Atwill, and *King of the Jungle* (1933), which starred Buster Crabbe. In 1970 Wylie wrote the "Los Angeles: A.D. 2017" episode of *Name of the Game*. Other scripts were written under Wylie's tutelage, but after a few disagreements and disenchantments, Wylie became less and less involved with Hollywood film makers. Nonetheless, the involvement with Hollywood had broadened his experience and opened up new vistas for future writing, to say nothing about the economic remuneration received for film adaptations of his work. These included Paramount's *Come on Marines* (1933), Twentieth-Century Fox's *Fair Warning* (1937), and *Springtime in the Rockies* (1942), Warner Brothers' *Cinderella Jones* (1946) and *Night Unto Night* (1949), and Paramount's *When Worlds Collide* (1951). In 1955-56, NBC filmed but never ran a television series based on and titled from the Crunch and Des series. In all, Wylie gained much experience, fame, and money from Hollywood throughout his career, though he had stopped actively writing specifically for the movies by the late Thirties.

Finnley Wren (1934)

Wylie's next book established two things: that Philip Wylie could write a successful philosophical novel, and that he was not afraid to experiment with style and subject matter. *Finnley Wren* raised Wylie's stock about ten points. The critics responded angrily to his use of sexually-explicit subject matter and words, as well as his literary exhibitionism. But the book was, and remains, one of Wylie's richest, most energetic, colorful, and poignantly thoughtful novels. It was Wylie's first true philosophical novel, vigorous in character and invigorating in action. What's more, it, more than any other of Wylie's novels to that point, revealed the author's awareness of and reaction to the pain and suffering caused by man's inhumanity to man.

Philip Wylie's vituperative style graphically emerged in this experimental novel of American manners in the Thirties. In *Finnley Wren* are "his notions and opinions together with a haphazard history of his career and amours in these moody years, as well as sundry rhymes, fables, diatribes and literary misdemeanors." This "novel in a new manner" is a *tour de force* written with a combination of satire, romance, pathos, and light humor. Billed as "a book in the spirit of Sterne and Rabelais," the novel is actually the account of Finnley Wren's life as told to Philip Wylie, the fictional author-narrator.

The novel is a colorful account of the times, sometimes sensational, often painful, an overview of life, a record of the loves, failures, and successes of Finnley Wren, a modern man in a frustrating and cruel modern world. Wren is humane, rebellious, unfettered by pretense, and free. Although an intellectual, he is neither unimaginative nor insipid, but an alive, feeling, thinking human being. Wren is, in short, Wylie's alter-ego, a character who represents the whole man, not the segmented and unintegrated man of the modern age, but the fully functioning Jungian personality. Wren's weekend story, from frightening childhood through emotional adulthood, provides exceptionally good insight into the author himself.

The action begins in a New York speakeasy with a chance meeting of Finnley Wren and Philip Wylie, who immediately strike up a conversation. Amid the noisy backdrop of drink, Finnley Wren begins his tale. "Thrust from the bloody bowels of woman and driven into the black, perpetual hiding place called death—with little between but blood and women and solitude— said Finnley Wren, drawing a line on the tablecloth with his knife—sometimes I am so terrified of life that I come near putting an end to it as a boon to my dreadful little nerves" (FW, p.3). Thus, the tone is set for the forty-eight-hour sojourn of the two men.

Finnley's life had begun on January 1, 1900. Son of a well-respected yet sadistic surgeon, he learned early of life's pains, hypocrisies, and frustrations. The physical and psychological brutality of his father was but one influence on the vulnerable child. Other painful incidents included the shattering of love's illusion by an early adolescent sweetheart, a paternity suit by a lower class girl who was actually several months pregnant when she met the young boy.

The drinking and storytelling continues as the two men move on to another speakeasy. Here the narrator learns of Finnley's difficulty gaining acceptance by his first wife's family. The bitter-sweet story continues until Finnley realizes he has an engagement at Donald Dwyer's country home in Connecticut. The narrator, whose own wife is on vacation, agrees to accompany Finnley for the weekend. The story shifts to the Dwyer estate where liberated men and women who are present provide the narrator with more information about the enigmatic Finnley. The narrator is eventually seduced by Flora, who appears to be an empty-headed blond, but is actually Mrs. Dwyer, a world famous obstetrician; and he later discovers that the Dwyer's party is really an experimental study in marriage, monogamy, sex, and jealousy done purely "in the interest of science."

From the weekend blitz to the end of the story, the narrative is an exposition of Finnley's life story. Wylie learns of several horrible and tragic episodes in Finnley's life, all of which are laced with the strong notions and opinions of real-life author Philip Wylie. The story ends in New York Central Station, and when the two men say good-by after their forty-eight hour sojourn, Wylie perceives a change in Finnley's personality. Later, Finnley calls Wylie, reaffirming the narrator's beliefs, and here the story abruptly ends.

One critic questioned whether the story was actually Rabelaisian. "Rabelais," he jeered, "would roar himself hoarse at the information that all this fiddle-faddle about copulation and all this wish fulfillment writing had anything to do with his abbey of his ilk." But Keefer points out, *Wren* is the "natural successor of *Heavy Laden* and *Babes and Sucklings*," which, though "causing a small furor when they appeared," are actually mild by today's standards, and "have been quietly forgotten. . .but Finnley Wren lives on. . ." (PW, p.66).

Finnley Wren is the first indication of Wylie's capacity for vehement outpourings. It is obvious that many of the events in the book are autobiographical, with Wylie's father Edmund, his first wife Sally, and others making distinctive appearances. Finnley's experience with the young woman who accuses him of fathering her child is taken directly from a similar incident which occurred in Wylie's life, bringing bitter opprobrium and shame to the Wylie household.

The novel itself combines harsh tirades with imaginative romance. Wren is a complex character. He is a feeling, thinking, and thoroughly human being who is revealed piece by piece in his own complexity. A typically Wylian character, he is detached, skeptical, and concerned with truth above all else. Wren's life is one of constant trial, similar to a soap opera, but more believable. Yet there is old-style heroism in Wren's personality, the type of heroism reserved for men who are larger than life, gutsy, living without concern for concensus, and generally "rollicking."

Although Wylie "bursts forth with a little of the vitality of Rabelais himself," wrote Mary McCarthy, "and although the reader will find a 'prodigiality' with words, he [Wylie] lacks 'literary taste'." In the most dramatic moments, he "stoops to a sensationalism which is as vulgar as anything Tiffany Thayer ever employed to titillate the public." The book was thus relegated to secondary importance by most critics, although the richness and liveliness were strong enough to enable most readers to overlook Wylie's occasional vulgarity and sensationalism.

The most outstanding feature of *Finnley Wren* is characterization. Through Wren, Wylie is able to express the ordinary in extraordinary ways, and the old mundanities of life are freshly drawn by the author's new approach to old perceptions. William Rose Benet summed up the general critical response: "Mr. Wylie can write. There is no doubt about that. After he gets through his sophomore year in letters, he may quite possibly do a novel 'as is' a novel." Benet points out that Wylie's criticism of modern civilization is valid in that Wylie's thinking is his own, and that Wylie's next book should be great. This one, he concludes, is not.

Miscellaneous Writing (1935-1943)

Wylie concentrated on "boiler makers" for the eight years between *Finnley Wren* and *Generation of Vipers*. During this period his "prodigious" output included "Movie scripts written in Hollywood, serialized novels in the best-paying magazines, a succession of murder mysteries, and finally the Crunch and Des series in *Saturday Evening Post*. . ." (PW, p.76). According to Keefer, Wylie would have been rich "if he had not spent the money as fast as it came in." For chronological purposes, Wylie's work in these years included *The Smiling Corpse* (published anonymously in 1935), several novels for *Redbook*, including *One Love at a Time* (1935; reprinted in 1936 as *As They Reveled*), *Too Much of Everything* (1936 in both serial and book form), *Second Honeymoon* (for *Redbook*, 1936), *Smoke Across the Moon* (1937 serial for *Saturday Evening Post*), *Home from the Hills* (for *Redbook* in 1937), and *No Scandal* (for *Redbook* in 1940).

The Crunch and Des stories began in 1939. "Widow Voyage," published in *Saturday Evening Post* on June 10, 1939, was the first of many adventure stories featuring the likeable Crunch Adams and Des(perate) Smith. Several book-length collections of stories starring these two Florida charter-boat operators appeared later, including *The Big Ones Get Away* (1940), *Salt Water Daffy* (1941), *Fish and Tin Fish* (1944), *Crunch and Des* (1948), and *Treasure Cruise* (1956). These stories continually brought praise from the critics, who felt that the author was eager to provide realistic, purely entertaining stories. "Each new chapter," wrote one critic about *Salt Water Daffy*, "is as exhilarating as a fresh cast." The characters, wrote another, are "a treasure of entertainment." It was hard to believe that the same man who wrote these delightful tales of fishing off the Florida Keys could so furiously explode in his other books. Wylie's Crunch and Des work eventually amounted to fifty-nine stories for *Saturday Evening Post*, plus seven 35,000-word novelettes, and about forty stories which were never published; and although these tales are clearly minor Wylie, they are still remembered fondly by his readers.

Too Much of Everything (1936); *An April Afternoon* (1938)

Too Much of Everything (1936) was both a prelude of things to come and an interesting look back. It dramatizes the Bentlan family's fall from riches to rags in the stock market crash of 1929. The story line follows the struggle of father William Bentlan, an ex-millionaire, as he tries to re-establish the inner values of his materialistic family. Mother Della, a social parasite, daughter Daphne, a fast girl who is able to drink and debauch with the best, son Jim, who is volatile and aggressive, and May, Iris, and Junior all give up their materialistic orientations, though not without a struggle, thus reaffirming the basis of the family. The disaster is in the end a teaching tool which helps the family regain their spiritual center.

This is one of Wylie's weakest novels, overly sentimental, lacking any real interpretative value. One critic has pointed out that it is the "product" of Wylie's own inner turmoil and inner questioning. If this novel is the ripple effect from self-evaluation in psychologically hard times, then this perhaps explains Wylie's sudden shift from advocate of a new morality to a much more conservative position. In any case, literary virtues are just not present in this book: the characters lack development; the style is choppy; the dialogue is unnatural and forced. The most successful aspect of the story is the description of financial disaster. The reunification of the family, though somewhat positive and idealistic, leaves the story pithy. Wylie's ability to perceive and write about the inner turmoil of tragedy had always been apparent; in this book it is his own ambivalence about life's spiritual meaning that stands out.

Throughout the Thirties Wylie continued to internalize anger about America's irresponsibility, its idiotic behavior patterns, its economic short-sightedness, its sexual repression and child-rearing stupidities. This anger simmered for a while, but in *An April Afternoon* (1938) it came to a complete boil.

An April Afternoon repeats the story of a thoroughly modern American family beset with difficulty, though in this case the difficulty is marital, not economic. This is the story of the Sheffield family, told from the perspective of their adopted son Frankie. The Sheffields are a modern family with a "let-it-all-hang-out" morality. They are, in contemporary jargon, open and authentic, able to confront any crisis with directness rather than evasion. This works most of the time, but when mother Connie runs away with a lover, abandoning family and husband, the group's response is not as high-minded as it might have been—their condemnation is an indication of a flaw in thoroughly modern morality. The family uses many philosophical "systems" in trying to understand the flaw in its thinking. In the end, the conflict is resolved when Connie Sheffield returns to and is accepted by her family.

Critical response to this occasionally over-dramatized novel was fairly good. Wylie's dash and wit was observed by one critic, who kindly commented that there was "not a dull moment in the story." Others responded to the writerly qualities and "craftsmanship" that made the story "thoroughly readable." Keefer feels that the book is "equal to or better than any of Wylie's novels," and brings out a chronologically important point. Wylie's conclusion that freedom must be tempered with self-restraint was a derivative of Jungian ideas. The characters failed to live up to their modern moral code because it "disregarded the fact that man is a creature whose actions are dominated by his feelings and his instinctual nature" (PW, p.93). Wylie would continue this line of reasoning with vigor in *Generation of Vipers* and *Essay on Morals*.

Philip Wylie's early years (1928-1942) reflected an America that was rapidly moving into a new era, of transition and of rapidly changing values, characterized by some uncertainty about national identity. The growth of technology and ascendency of industry, the movement from a rural to urban culture, and new scientific discoveries combined to pressure traditional American values. All of this was reflected in Wylie's early work.

His first books, from *Heavy Laden* to *Too Much of Everything*, chronicled his own changing values. They allowed him to crystallize his opinions and attitudes, experiment with different literary forms, and slowly develop basic literary skills. He could always tell a convincing tale, but now he was able to create evocative images through subtle and sensitive description, believable and fully developed characters. Wylie reached his maturity with *Finnley Wren*, and was, by the early Forties, ready to emerge as the major social force that he felt he was. Ironically, the next ten years would be dominated by his critical essays and nonfiction, and it would be his polemics which would catapult him into world renown.

CHAPTER III:
The Philosophical Works

By the Forties, the growth of the American middle-class was manifest. Finding its roots in American business, this new mass, worshipping material objects, seemed to believe that the business of America was business. Sinclair Lewis's George F. Babbitt epitomized this new American ethic. America, it seemed, was filled with Zenith Cities, populated by chauvinistic, bigoted, "manly men, womanly women, and bright kids" whose false sense of values represented Americana at its worst.

This is the America that Philip Wylie attacked in *Generation of Vipers*, his "catalogue" of what he felt was morally, spiritually, and intellectually wrong with his countrymen. "Dashed off" between the twelfth of May and fourth of July in 1942, this unbridled diatribe against America caused an unexpected furor and made Wylie famous overnight. It remains Wylie's most recognized work, and one of the most controversial books of the century. Its rise to best-seller status surprised no one more than the author himself.

Generation of Vipers is more brazen than brilliant, certainly not Wylie at his best. Nonetheless, it gave birth to a whole phenomenon, and set the stage for his future nonfiction and fiction alike. When he felt that the public misunderstood *Vipers*, Wylie, four years later, wrote another splenetic survey of American values. *An Essay on Morals*, no less important than *Vipers*, represents a second stage in Wylie's philosophical development. A third polemic, *The Magic Animal: Mankind Revisited*, was published in 1968, and represents the final stage in his thought. All three are religious in nature; all three reflect Wylie's understanding of Jungian theory.

There is without question a need to evaluate Wylie's underlying philosophy as it developed and changed throughout his career. And although his ideas are best understood within a developmental chronology, this chapter, by necessity, will momentarily break from the historical progression. *The Magic Animal*, though appearing in 1968, represented a change in Wylie's thinking, and must be considered in relationship to the previous two polemics. The chronology will continue with Wylie's fiction in the next chapter. It is necessary to view the later novels with a clear understanding of Wylie's conceptual ideas.

Generation of Vipers (1943)

If the first third of the twentieth century was marked by uncertainty, the second third was equally marked by anxiety. Scientific discovery at the turn of the century had effectively changed the pervading beliefs about man and the universe. Discoveries by Planck, Einstein, and Heisenberg forever destroyed the Newtonian mechanistic view of the universe, and relativity had undermined man's confidence in his ability to know anything. Freud's discovery of irrational, unconscious drives within man that were stronger than conscious, rational motives compounded the problem. The idea that man could depend on his rationality to solve all problems was in serious jeopardy. Civilization, by repressing primitive instinctual lusts and fears, was itself the primary cause of collective and individual neurosis, which would inevitably, wrote Freud, be expressed through intense nationalism and war.

Wylie was familiar with Freudian theories. His personal research into dynamic psychology lead to an unusually clear understanding of both Freud and Jung. By 1940, he had already begun expounding these ideas in his magazine writing. Articles such as "Worried About Yesterday," written for *Good Housekeeping* in October, 1941, attempted to translate such esoteric notions into readable tips for the layman. These articles discussed basic concepts such as "projection," "repression," and "instinct," giving often over-simplified but sound advice. Taking difficult concepts and translating them into the language of everyman, Wylie alienated university pedants, but slowly gathered a following of middle Americans.

Freud's theories were at the basis of Wylie's early thought. The motivating drives of the unconscious mind, the nature of true reality, repression of basic urges, dreams, fantasies, and collective neuroses were all questioned in the early novels. If reason and rationality were subordinate to the primary forces that lurk in the unconscious, and if what men repress reveals itself later in some other form, then, reasoned Wylie, we need an honest appraisal of our moral concerns. This he did through his fiction, where he constantly addressed the inevitable moral tension between society's demands and the instinctual, unconscious, primitive part of man. Human nature and civilization seemed, to Wylie, to be antithetical, yet forever locked together.

Wylie believed that man's instinctual nature was a higher good. Yet, religious and other institutionalized ego deceptions refused to accept the fact that man is an animal, that man has animal instincts, and that this is fundamentally good. Searching for his own definition of man, Wylie reasoned that Freud was correct, and that the principles which explained the actions of animals would equally explain those of man. Even the war itself could be explained through the paradoxical collective wish for self-destruction, and nationalism could be explained as the irrational transference of repressed sexual and lustful yearnings from natural parents to surrogate authority.

The real influence behind the writing of *Generation of Vipers* was far simpler than Freudian and Jungian psychology. Wylie was motivated by the unconscious state of his country.. Having recently completed a stint in the government information service, Wylie, in 1942, was ill, discouraged, and frustrated with American apathy toward the war effort. Taking his wife's advice on how to calm himself, he cathartically put his feelings on paper. After six weeks of furious writing, the feelings were out, and he had given birth to the famous book.

Generation of Vipers was a blockbuster. The reception was nothing less than phenomenal. Helped by some pre-publication publicity from Walter Winchell, who had raved about the book on an evening radio show, the first edition of the book sold out quickly. Philip Wylie received national prominence, much praise and plenty of criticism. Upon reaching national prominence, Wylie was overwhelmed, but ready for fame and fortune.

In most of his previous books, Wylie had taken positions similar to those he now took in *Generation of Vipers*, but here he spelled them out more forcefully, without the guise of fiction.

Vipers was a straightforward compilation of vociferous essays attacking religion, science, sexual values, women, scientists, businessmen, military men, doctors, statesmen, educators, and more. It was, in short, an attack on the whole of American values. For all its fury and negativeness, the book invited Americans to build a better world through objective criticism and constructive change. Wylie wanted to build a better America, but few saw the book in this light, opting instead to see the author as an iconoclastic crusader or "God's Angry Man." Realistically, he was neither. He was, rather, the conscience of the nation, or, as he would later describe himself, "God's little archer."

The book contained some painful truths and more than its share of shaky generalizations. Wylie's America was "hypocritical, lying, cheating, sex-crazed, advertising, doped, whimpering, soft, and insanely governed." It was a society of men who worked hard to earn money to give to the women, who were then duped by other men into purchasing needless gadgets and devices. It was a society of women who used their sexuality to gain favors from the men, who were sex-starved and disillusioned. It was a society where young women were trained to search for, find, and eventually reject their prince charming. The book left no stone unturned, attacked all aspects of Americana, and provided few answers. Closer to a "hell and damnation" sermon than a logical delineation of a particular position, this catalogue of "sin and moral desuetude" was the author's first nonfiction book, and as such demands close attention.

Although there are many reasons for the failure of American society, there are, writes Wylie, two central problems, immediately perceptible. Science and religion have failed society. While the former has overlooked man's subjective domain, the latter has preoccupied itself with superficial form and ritual. Neither has contributed to the betterment of mankind, and neither is concerned with "a general increase in the consciousness of man." Science, perverting its own methodology, is devoted to uselessly increasing worldly goods and gadgets, and religion is wrapped up in its own dogmatic institutions. Wylie, always an ardent believer in "true science," suggests that a new approach to human problems be taken, one that maintains strict scientific objectivity in relationship to subjective man. This approach must, he writes, "pursue the truth and truth only, because all else is by definition false." Since the cause of all human problems, in Wylie's opinion, comes from within man himself, and because "the millennium will come only when the average man exhibits a scientific integrity about all he is and does," the remainder of the book takes great pains to reveal the American brand of self-deception. It points out that Americans, though convinced of their civilized nature, are actually "still medieval—cruel bumpkins and dancing savages."

Using an approach that would become common in his later fiction, Wylie, in the second chapter, hypothesizes what future historians' accounts of 1940 will be like. This sometimes frightening, sometimes ridiculous account includes, among other things, commentary on sports, novels, promiscuity, colleges, law, the arts, and other activities of "the average medieval man," a species which "a modern geneticist would not let breed, and a meat inspector would not let pass." Titled "Subjective Feudalism," this chapter serves as an appetizer for what follows.

Wylie displays his bias early in the book. The ultimate solution is to be found in Jungian psychology. Although he would write another book, further clarifying the Jungian approach, Wylie, in *Vipers*, boldly argues a case for the rightness of man's animal instinctual nature. The answer to the question of man's destiny can be discovered by anyone willing to combine the Socratic dictate of "know thyself" (*gnothi se auton*) with Jungian concepts of instinct, myth, and the collective unconscious. Throughout the remainder of the book, his arguments attack man's stubborn refusal to admit either to his animal nature, his personification of instincts, or his creation of myths through universal archetypes. The result of this willful ignorance: dysfunction between man's physical and spiritual nature.

Wylie spends the next three chapters describing and analyzing a specimen American "myth," a specimen American "attitude," and a specimen American "institution." Each, according to Wylie, represents a fundamental error in American philosophy. Each can be explained in Jungian terms. These chapters were the basis of much criticism. Critics alleged that Jung's thought had been seriously distorted, charges that Wylie vociferously denied.

Taking the legend of Cinderella as a specimen American myth, Wylie points out that the American Cinderella is a perversion of an original wonderful story. The original Cinderella myth emphasized the molding of character through adversity and the discovery of a proper mate "in the dross and discard" of life. In the American version the prince's difficult search is eliminated, as is the importance of adversity as a precondition for virtue. The American version of the myth virtually eliminates any understanding of process. Instead, the emphasis falls on the girl's reward, which has come to be expected rather than earned. American women, writes Wylie, "expect the reward of the soft life because society at one time believed that the bearing of children was such an unnatural and hideous ordeal that the mere act entitled women respite from all other physical and social responsibility." This, comments Wylie, is the cause for the defeat of "half the husbands in America." Further, when Cinderella discovers that her prince charming is just an ordinary husband, she makes his life miserable, and soon becomes a "mom."

Wylie's famous chapter on "common women" takes issue with mom, "the inevitable result—and creator—of Cinderella." When Cinderella discovers that her husband is no prince after all, she metamorphosizes into "the puerile, rusting, raging creature we know as mom." Wylie challenges our reverence and adulation of this "middle-aged puffin with an eye like a hawk that has just seen a rabbit twitch far below." He writes that although there has been "filial duty by many sorts of civilizations, it is only in America where an entire division of living men has been used, during wartime, or at any time, to spell out the word 'mom' on a drillfield." Wylie concludes his tirade by saying that women have been replaced in usefulness by the machine, and stripped of biological possibilities by time. Yet they feel they deserve respect, try to meddle in world affairs, and expect to be catered to. Actually, writes Wylie, women "possess some 80% of the nation's money," spending it on oafish machines and the radio, which is "mom's soul," her "final tool for it stamps everybody who listens with the matriarchal brand." Wylie continues: "Just as Goebbels has revealed what can be done with such a mass stamping of the public psyche in his nation, so our land is a living representation of the same fact worked out in matriarchal sentimentality, goo, slop, hidden cruelty, and the foreshadow of national death."

While Wylie's choice for the specimen American "attitude" is that of sexuality, the specimen American "institution" is education. Both violate man's instinctual nature. The former ignores man's animal sexual nature, which is instinctual, and which if denied will reveal itself in various forms of neurosis and hysteria. The latter ignores what is important—the ability to think critically—and focuses instead on "facts," which themselves are questionable. In fact, Wylie points out, literacy in America is at such a low level that his statements will not even be intelligible to millions of Americans.

Wylie's next target is the myth of the common man, whom he considers the "hero's backside," the class which has caused most of the problems in the nation. His approach to the problem of the "Common Man" is more a discussion of Jung's "Law of Opposites" than anything else. The "Law of Opposites" is to psychology what the second law of thermodynamics is to physics. Action and reaction apply to the psyche as well as to physical objects. In formulating any type of moral value structure, one must consider the problem of opposites, for nothing is ever activated in isolation. The common man must be educated to the conflicting emotions within. Only then will he stop projecting his own inadequacies on other men. Wylie's observations about personality are similar to those found in Adorno's study of the authoritarian personality.

The remainder of the book takes issue with "uncommon men": scientists, medical doctors, businessmen, statesmen, professors, congressmen, military men, and finally "the Man on the Cross" himself. This second to last chapter reveals Wylie's evidence for a religious answer to the problems discussed previously. The cure, "to know thyself," is an ancient one. All of the major religious and philosophical figures have said this, from Christ to Buddha. This chapter is a justification of Wylie's entrenched beliefs. Inner honesty and candor must be held above all else if truth and self-knowledge are to be achieved. "It has been fairly fancy of me," concludes Wylie, "to write so long and noisy a book just to say that if we want a better world we will have to be better people." This was Christ's message, and like "the man on the cross," Wylie is calling for private integrity.

Despite his claims to the contrary, Wylie's solution is essentially religious. Knowing oneself through critical analysis and self-discipline is a religious idea. By eliminating dogma and scrutinizing the self, truth will manifest itself: this is, after all, what "the founding fathers said; all Christ said; all there is to say." Wylie concludes by discussing the ultimate product of the truthful search: a true understanding of freedom and democracy. America had tremendous potential, and now, amidst a war, "Never was chaos so great. Never was paradise so near to the reach of common folks—like you, and clowns—like me."

Generation of Vipers had an enormous impact on its times. From Taylor Caldwell to Walter Winchell, everyone had read this controversial new book. The popular market was buzzing; the critics were a little confused. Wylie already had a reputation for flouting established ideas, but this explosion went well beyond what was expected. The controversy spread. Sales averaged about five thousand copies per year, with total sales reaching 180,000 in cloth by 1954. When the author invited his readers to correspond with him, he was deluged by over ten thousand letters in the first year alone. Wylie had fortuitously uncovered what the public had been looking for— a chance to vicariously blow off a little steam.

Critical response was mixed. The book was described as a "tub-thumping diatribe against American customs." Reviewers jeered at Wylie's less than profound claim "that we'd better begin improving our world by first improving ourselves." An affronted Paul Stringer protested that not even the "smallest point, relative or not, is passed without unfavorable comment: Washington—a woman chaser; Grant—a drunk; Lincoln—a mug; the Pilgrims—bums." And someone, he retorted, should explain to Mr. Wylie that "these gentlemen do not belong to this generation of vipers; unfortunately, they are dead."

Thomas Sugrue, critic for the *New York Herald Tribune*, credited Wylie for writing a "truly remarkable book," one magnificent in its own arrogance, entertaining, amusing, and irritating. "It should be kept in a cool place," he concluded. Similarly, *Time Magazine*'s reviewer pointed out that Wylie's "religious perceptions are rudimentary," and that his "prose ranges between brilliant neo-Menckenism and embarrassing vulgarity." Most critics and reviewers exposed Wylie's inconsistencies and absurdities, taking issue with his use of words, his outrageous attacks, his irreverence. But few, if any, could deny the points he made on American mores. Wylie's accusation that these enumerated faults got the United States into the war and would "lose us the peace" were truthful observations, but, as pointed out by most readers, these same faults also got us into democracy and had always been causes of war and peace throughout history.

Wylie succeeded in shattering illusion and pretense. Keefer comments that Wylie "became a legend in his own time" for three reasons: (1) people with less courage and ability to express themselves could, through Wylie's intrepidness, vicariously share his feelings; (2) Wylie exposed those elements of Americana that had mesmerized people into giving them false respect, and the public would not soon be fooled again; (3) Wylie leaped over the bonds of propriety with "unrestrained ferocity," both shocking and impressing the public.

And, Wylie would continue to preach. The words from which the book's title was taken remain the best description of his concern: "All manner of sin and blasphemy shall be given unto men; but blasphemy against the spirit shall not be forgiven—whosoever speaketh against the eternal truth in the spirit of men, it shall not be forgiven him, neither in this world, neither in the world to come—Either make the tree good, and his fruit good; or else make the tree corrupt, and his fruit corrupt; for the tree is known by his fruit."

O generation of vipers—!

For the rest of his career he would seek to expose the blasphemies of spiritual truth. He would try to make the tree and the fruit good, and would be ridiculed and attacked for it. Ultimately, he would fail, but not before reiterating his ideas in myriad articles, essays, stories, and books.

Hero and villain, Philip Wylie was now in demand. Who was he? Why did he write with such vehemence? Where did he come from? In a "not too-reverent sketch of his career as author and critic" (appearing in the August,

1944, issue of *Publisher's Weekly*), he describes himself as a sensitive and collapsible person, whose "status neuroticus" is such that "almost anything has the power to shatter" him. Rejecting the image of crusader, fighter, liberal, or even hack, Wylie, who felt that nothing could be further from the truth, explains that his life resembles a "spoke-like series of experiments in escape with each new spoke proving itself a gauntlet." Denying any unusual courage, he asserts that he acts for social change because "when a man can run no farther, he must stand and fight." Wylie then closes the autobiography, describing himself as a "portable nervous wreck—ex-rotarian, former government official, angler, and typical middle-class American."

This is an odd autobiography for anyone, even Philip Wylie. One can only assume that he combined tongue-in-cheek with his new confidence. If Philip Wylie was a mystery, the philosophical framework of his work was not. His magazine publications after *Generation of Vipers* made his aims and motives quite clear.

Ardent patriotism persisted in all of his work. Regardless of his criticisms, Wylie believed in supporting his country in war and peace. "War and Peace in Miami," appearing in *The New Republic* in 1944, exemplified this. In it he takes issue with the tourist industry in Miami Beach, a place where those enlisted men "who have sacrificed most" meet "those who have sacrificed least," the tourist. Squeezing money out of the serviceman was perfidious enough, but disallowing soldiers their much-needed rest and relaxation after fighting was traitorous. The fact that tourists felt free to drive to Miami, using gasoline that could have contributed to America's war effort, was, concludes Wylie, just another example of Americans failing "to understand, even vaguely, the meaning of these days."

In addition to his free-lance articles, Wylie used the "Strictly Personal" column in *The Saturday Review of Literature* as a forum for his criticism of American values. If the period from 1929-1939 reflected a mood of disappointment in America—and the war years were grievously disappointing—the post-war years, prognosticated Wylie in "More Footnotes on the Cinderella Story," reflected a pronounced condition of "pre-disappointment." Why? Americans, answers Wylie, reared on the Cinderella lie of rags to riches, expected to "get nearly everything for next to nothing"; and because the myth was so embedded in the American psyche, the people would never realize that glass slippers do not promote locomotion.

Furthermore, writes Wylie in another war-related article, "diplomats, politicians, and tycoons can utter such gruesome nonsense and blunder whole continents into war" only because they never learned how to think. Why? Educators are illiterate. This, he went on, is unmistakable to anyone exposed "to the basic material of contemporary learning" written by so-called skilled professors. If we can curtail the publication of doctoral theses and publish textbooks anonymously, we might, he concludes, eliminate "books compounded of pretty erudition and ambitious vacuum of obscurantism and illiteracy—books written under duress."

Wylie also attacked private interests, intellectual liberals, and the facts of war. He proclaims that U. S. leadership was a "muddy, mixed-up war of people who don't know enough, led by people who thought they knew everything." He points out that the United States had lost its sense of values, and was fighting for reasons other than "preserving that for which all of us stand." There are, claims Wylie, only a few Americans who understand the conscious symbols of individual dignity for each man and woman and child there and everywhere.

"Sex and the Censor," written for *The Nation*, argues that censorship of obscenity "is the work of the impure, to whom all things are impure," and that "banning a book is the same as burning it." But, writes Wylie in an energetic attack, the most guilty party in banning books is organized religion—primarily the Catholic and Protestant churches. They, he goes on, have the right to question laws and rules, but not to demand and impose. These "hysterical zealots", especially in a time of war, can betray the common sense of a whole people. These same people, he concludes, are the ones who got us into the war and need to be stopped, "both in the name of truth and of democracy."

In the mid-Forties, Wylie wrote myriad articles and essays. His articles included such diverse topics as "All I Know About Banks" (*Saturday Review*), "I Found Out a Little About Polio," (*Saturday Evening Post*), "Memorandum on Anti-Semitism" (*American Mercury*), and many others, including such titles as "More Musings on Mom," "What's Wrong with American Marriages," and "How Are Your Illusions?". Two articles, "Deliverance or Doom" and "Safe and Insane," were concerned with atomic energy and weaponry, a new area of interest for the country and Wylie. In addition to these articles, several books and stories were written.

Although *Generation of Vipers* was a blockbuster, Wylie inadvertently damaged his credibility by ending the book the way he did. Describing himself as a "clown," he misled many readers into believing the book to be a "put on." Troubled by this and the charge that he himself did not understand Jung's theories, Wylie wrote his second nonfiction book, *An Essay on Morals*, primarily as an explication of Jungian theory and as a demonstration of his own seriousness.

An Essay on Morals (1947)

An Essay on Morals was a prodigious undertaking. Its subtitle gives an indication of the scope of the work: "A science of philosophy and a philosophy of the sciences; a popular explanation of the Jungian theory of human instincts; a new bible for the bold mind and a way to personal peace by logic; the heretic's handbook and text for honest skeptics, including a description of man suitable for an atomic age, together with a compendium of means to brotherhood in a better world and a voyage beyond the opposite directions of religion of objective truth, to understanding." And there you are, wrote one critic, all for two dollars and a half!

An Essay on Morals was Wylie's definitive philosophical statement. Written with typically inflamed rhetoric and obscure language, the book was incomprehensible to many and bewildering to most. Described by one critic as "a secondary school course, conducted by the author in a loud voice," the book is best described as popular philosophy. It was not well-received, with the most frequent criticisms aimed at the author's apparent misunderstanding of Jung, his lack of philosophical sophistication, and his disregard for the scientific method. This enraged Wylie, who, in 1951, rewrote the preface to the book to provide a firmer thread for understanding the essay.

The new preface was Wylie's response to the critics, as well as his statement of purpose. In it he attempts to show that he was "neither angry nor bewildered" when he wrote the essay. Refusing to apologize for using uncommon vocabulary, he points out that neither physicists, lawyers, nor theologians are asked to confine their ideas to the common argot, yet he, a writer and thinker, is. "I am trying to tell about the science of psychology," he responds, "not about Studs Lonigan." What's more, Jung himself had written to Wylie, praising both his approach and his explanation of the esoteric theory. "So those academic philosophers, pedants and reviewers," huffs Wylie, "who contend that this volume shows my 'ignorance' of Jung are, merely, themselves uninformed—and pitifully so."

What was Wylie's understanding of Jungian psychology and how does it apply to *An Essay on Morals* and the rest of his work? The belief that man is an animal is the central point. To understand Jung, Wylie writes, "man must be thought of as an animal, simply—the present end-product of evolving terrestrial life." Unfortunately, as Wylie points out in Chapter Two, "not one person in ten thousand accepted the discovery for the amazing truth that it represents." They either believe that man, created by God, is beyond instinct, or that man, a *tabula rasa* at birth, is instinctual and must be forcibly controlled. Neither is satisfactory to Wylie, whose moral system is based on the assurance that he and the good reader are "beasts" and "that we are nothing else."

Wylie's second proposition follows from the first. Man is an animal and animals are instinctual; therefore, man is governed by instinct. But, because man has developed an ego that cannot accept this, man chooses, rather, to believe that reason or will or some divine element guides action. Wylie suggests that reason is merely "an instrument of biology," and that "goodness" relates and flows from "the purpose of instinct" which conceals itself, allowing man to think he is divine. But, "awareness is the instinct of the instinct—their consciousness of themselves and of the material world." Chapters Four and Five deal with the biological and psychological evidences of instinct. While the former argues that from the moment of inception the human being "relives the history of his forebears," the latter presents Freud's concepts of unconscious sexual instincts, which Wylie considers the foundation for Jung's theories.

Wylie's third point is that instinct, in man, has taken the form of legend or myth. Because man uses symbols (his instincts require symbols), "he gradually personified them," with qualities of virtue taking on the form of "gods." As man became more sophisticated, so did these "archetypal images." Because the same symbols have appeared in all places and periods, and because legends are universally parallel, Jung, states Wylie, "concluded that the process of translating instinct into legend and legend into religion is *innate in man.*"

Jung, writes Wylie in Chapter Six, "suggests the term collective unconscious to describe instinct." Every religion unconsciously attempts to express these collective instincts, and, according to Jung, if all religions instantly disappeared, man would immediately begin to reconstruct deities and forces to explain those processes within and without, those forces which "drive him mad as an individual and hurl him into chaos as a nation if he much misuses or long misinterprets them." Chapters Six and Seven are concerned with further substantiation of man's instinctual nature and the psychological avoidance of it.

Denial of instinct is vanity. Man the egoist refuses "to recognize instincts because they are 'animal' in nature, and invents gods to hide that fact." Or, writes Wylie, man believes that logic, reason, and science make him superior to animals: "every egoist, religious or atheistic, has therefore lost touch with his instincts; they operate without his consciousness. . . and do not coincide with truth. Therefore, he is forced to rationalize his behavior."

Point four is that all persons have instincts which are arranged in contradictory pairs. This "law of opposites" governs all instinctual behavior, and, as Wylie stated in *Vipers*, this is the subjective equivalent of the law of thermodynamics. Instinct operates according to its own thermodynamics and laws of motion. Wylie's hypothesis is that compensation, complement, and conservation operate subjectively just as they do in the objective world. Hence, "for every instinct put to *conscious* use by man—or society—there exists a potential force, equal, opposed, and *unconscious* unless the individual (or the group) recognizes the dual nature of the instinct." An instinctual principle sets up its opposite liability, and unless we recognize the forces working within ourselves and the collectivity, we will unwittingly set the world in peril. Conscience is the best means of recognition. It is the organ of instinct which allows man to deal with subjective facts as honestly as he deals with objectivity in science.

The crisis in contemporary morality, reasons Wylie, is the result of the denial of subjectivity. This "inevitable consequence of a psychological law of compensation" has produced "world-wide hostility, rage, frustration, and fear" because we have concentrated solely on objects, ignoring the cost of losing the subjective sphere. Presenting examples of Russian materialists, German fascists, and the Christian church, Wylie argues his premise that the "law of opposites" operates in the collective sphere and "affects all alike."

Wylie's final discussion centers on the Jungian concept of transcendence, "which depends on the assimilation of the previous four ideas and upon the experiencing of the processes they represent." A person must be subjectively honest, "seeking within himself the constant operation of compensation." If one can discern his own instincts, make choices of action compatible with the "purpose of instinct," and come to an awareness of his total nature, transcendence will result. Transcendence is not a mystical experience, but "the experience which follows a large, new psychological enlightenment. . .analogous to the change in objective outlook and capacity which ensues upon education." When Wylie wrote that *An Essay on Morals* was essentially a religious work, this is what he was referring to. Transcendence, in Wylie's mind, has been the goal of religion.

The ultimate goal of *Morals* was to re-evaluate mankind's moral foundation, which was, to Wylie's thinking, based on the failure to admit, evaluate, and transcend instinct. Wylie called for his fellow man to re-embrace knowledgeably instinct through "adopting morals germane without sciences: Instinct, Conscience, the Collective Unconscious, the Paired and Opposite Archetypes we contain and represent, and the function of consciousness as it may be evolved by these." The remainder of the book merely supports and emphasizes these points. Wylie studies the instinctual condition of soldier, physicist, and priest, and after pointing out the idiocies of the former two, says of the latter: "I have been hard on the church. I would be harder; I would do away with it." The church, "this one more appalling institution in man's story," in all of its glorious history has served merely to shield man from his true nature. It is what "ego invents to spare itself from the sight of instinct," in spite of the damage it does to subjective health.

Wylie's conclusion is a call for truth, because "all truth is accessible to the truthful." In the future "we must return to work in the inner nature half of the time and work in the outer world only for the balance of our hours." Energy spent on "vicarious living—luxury and vanity—monotonously destroys us down the ages. And nine-tenths of the energy expended in America is for that. . .when the individual compromises with the moral order of instinct, he dies; and when many do it together, they die."

Morals represents a split with the "scientific method" with which Wylie was so enamoured in earlier years. The book was scorned by critics and reviewers, who objected to Wylie's unorthodox views of man and nature, poked fun at Wylie's "apparent" disregard for the history of philosophy, and railed at Wylie's misuse of logic. Monroe Beardsley, writing for *The Western Review*, described *Morals* as "popular philosophy" which would mislead those "moderately reflective" people who were not trained to read Aristotle, St. Thomas, Spinoza, Bradley, or Dewey. Furthermore, he quips, the author himself gets his ideas "at third hand and then pouts because he cannot understand the philosopher." He concluded that Wylie's readers would "pay through the nose in over-simplification of thought and confusion of purpose" in a book that has the tautological premise that "people's behavior patterns are caused by their behavior patterns."

Commonweal's Henry Beck condemned Wylie's failure to ever define "morality." Further objecting to Wylie's theories on the origin of religion, Beck commented that the attempt to shock and stun the Christian is stale air of the nineteenth century. More rancorous criticism came from *The New Republic*'s Fredric Wertham, who likened both Wylie and Jung to fascists, and pointed out that "Fascism, like this book, is a symptom of a disorder that cannot be cured by psychoanalysis." False rationalizations and ideologies perpetuate human wrongdoing, not instincts. Jungian psychology and Wylie's interpretation of it, he concluded, will keep people from looking for real causes and real remedies.

Unfortunately, *An Essay on Morals* is badly written. It is difficult to read, if not incomprehensible. As an expression of personal anger, it is assuredly honest, but also offensive and unintelligible. The critics were right. Wylie was far better at tearing down than reconstructing. No solutions were proposed; no answers were given. Accusing Wylie of "slick journalism," critics rightly argued that Wylie's pseudo-scientific bombast, "glib expressions," and "gassy notions" took away from any serious call for morality, obscured the subtlety of his thought, and betrayed his ideals. Even Wylie's supporters refused to let him off the hook. After a second reading of *Morals*, Morton Robinson, who had previously been a staunch supporter of Wylie's writing, grimly concluded that Wylie, "as a whip-master, is tremendous. . .but in the more difficult task of marshalling general ideas. . . Mr. Wylie's gifts fail him." Finally, Robinson concludes, "Mr. Wylie is not a thinker, he scares nobody, and helps nobody, when he tries to be one."

There are brilliant parts to *Morals*, but Wylie's own indignation obscured his thinking. Keefer correctly points out that *Morals* "was a success in spite of itself—but not the kind Wylie had intended" (PW, p.112). The critical uproar over Wylie's views on sex and religion "made it a celebrated work." It sold 61,862 copies in cloth. Ironically, in spite of all the objections, the controversial statements on sex and religion would be commonplace by the mid-Sixties. But "to say that this change all began with Wylie is to make an assertion which cannot be proved—but who can think that all those copies of *An Essay on Morals* had no impact?" (PW, p.112-113).

The Innocent Ambassadors (1957)

Although it would be over twenty years before Wylie would burst forth with another attempt to reassess mankind, a different type of nonfiction work came in the interim. *The Innocent Ambassadors* was written during and after a three-month trip abroad, which took the Wylies "to the Far East and India and brought them home with stopovers in Lebanon, Turkey, and Greece." This round-the-world travelogue was a combination vacation slide show and "compendium of data" not found in the run-of-the-mill guidebook. It included "candid autobiographical fragments" about the author and "biographical notes about the author's wife, a fine woman." And finally, "a survey of places, both exotic and troubled, undertaken in these terrifying times; along with diverse psychological observations, philosophical comments, horrid sights, vivid insights, assorted enjoyments, revelations, practical suggestions for the salvation of liberty, and sundry flights of fancy; in sum, a perfectly wonderful book that anyone would be fascinated to read."

Described by one critic as a "combination global travelogue, jeremiad on Communism, and valentine to Mrs. Wylie," this book, billed as a "round-the-world *Generation of Vipers*," is more than chit-chat and less than philosophy. It is well-intended, as were all of Wylie's books, but reveals subtle arrogance and subjectivism. Although his intention was to open American minds to the rest of the world (and his observations appear to be painfully accurate), his travel experience was undoubtedly colored by his own, subjectively biased predispositions. Communism was Wylie's particular bugaboo. Because Americans do not understand "what Communism is" and "fail to see the trap it has constructed around us," Wylie, in this book, felt compelled to warn them about the advance of tyranny and their failure to combat it. Americans, he writes, can no longer feel superior because they are white, and should begin propagandizing democratic beliefs in the Orient, which, he implies, will be the next battleground for freedom.

The book, in short, is a venturing-out for Philip Wylie. His earlier travel venture, a trip to Russia in 1936, had ended tragically. His half-brother had been killed—murdered, as Wylie saw it—while traveling through Poland. The 1957 trip had serious psychological and ideological importance to the author. There was, unfortunately, much truth in Wylie's observations. The Far East did become the next battleground for democracy, John Foster Dulles's foreign policies did create some difficulty, and "ugly Americanism" did present a nasty image of the United States to the rest of the world.

Most critics felt that the book was preachy and overloaded with personal philosophizing, which, they felt, obscured its positive aspects. Outside of the critic for *Atlantic*, who felt the book to be full of "corny posturing" and large amounts of "unconscious farce," most recommended that it be read. R. L. Duffus, reviewer for *The New York Times Book Review*, noted that *Ambassadors*, though at times "exasperating" and "dull," has "life enough in it to make it worth going through, and it does have a needed message of goodwill, from West to East." *Saturday Review*'s critic summed it up best when he took note of Wylie's coverage of Hawaii, Japan, China, India, and Lebanon, Wylie's "graphic reactions to the people, the food, the beauty, the horrors," and Wylie's "cerebrations" on their "religion, philosophy, and sex," likening his tirades to "parental scolding," and pointing out that this harshness is "motivated by his deep love for mom and the kids," or his intense patriotism.

The Magic Animal: Mankind Revisited (1968)

Eleven years passed before Wylie produced the definitive statement of his later years, a phase in his writing which would reveal his growing pessimism about the future of mankind's dream. Believing that he owed his readers a companion piece to *Generation of Vipers*, Wylie, in *The Magic Animal*, was determined to let the public know what he was *for*, what he thought about the world in 1968, and what he saw as a remedy for mankind's ills. He unabashedly proclaims in the prefatory note that he is for truth, reality, knowledge, learning, reason, insight, hope, art, excitement, and daydreaming, or, "love, in another way of saying." The dearest aim of Americans, progress, only comes about through criticism, and this was his practice, regardless of the public's response. His earlier books were criticized for providing no tangible remedy to the problems that he pointed to. This infuriated Wylie, who accused his critics of semi-thought. Perception of mistakes and solutions do not necessarily come about simultaneously. Technologically advanced people should know this. Nevertheless, *The Magic Animal*, two years in the making, would try to re-educate the public.

The Magic Animal represents the third and final stage in Wylie's philosophical development. Here he draws from biological naturalists rather than from psychologists. The book continues the argument that man is an animal with animal instincts, provides further evidence that religion should be done away with, and, for all purposes, takes up where *Generation of Vipers* and *An Essay on Morals* left off. There is, however, one difference. In the quarter of a century that had passed since the appearance of *Vipers* groups of men had "found more facts about our species," and Wylie, having kept up with those facts, was determined to demonstrate the implications of this new "wealth of information." With these newly discovered facts, writes Wylie, to continue believing in our traditional "concepts of god, Nature, and Man" is "as mistaken and as provably mistaken" as to continue believing that the earth is flat. This book would show "how man came to be and what the specialists now know he is." Its goal: to help produce a "religion" that allows "every mind to change its beliefs each time a new truth or a truer truth indicates that duty."

Wylie opens with a revision of Genesis. The true beginning was matter and motion. There was no life. Earth was a "stable star." Life arose because "it is a property of matter that appears under suitable conditions and evolves while such conditions persist." The mystery of life is no more: its evolution was inevitable. Bathed in the energy of the sun, chemicals mixed and altered, growing more and more complex. Hundreds and millions of years passed, and "a special cell emerged in the pungent broths of the ocean or a lake. It had being; it ate food; it divided and so reproduced. It was alive and it was life. Nothing important remains secret about its origin."

There is no mystery about it. There is no kindly old man with a beard sculpting man from clay and woman from rib. The evolution of the species, wrote Wylie, was just as inevitable. "Slowly, by those infrequent, random changes and the survival of the rare mutants with helpful differences, our ancestors evolved." Joseph Wood Krutch described accidental-but-helpful gene change as "invention of nature." Wylie, drawing on Krutch, claims that the most dazzling invention of nature was sex, which allowed for more genetic variation and greater numbers than simple cell division. This change "astronomically accelerated the evolutionary process," but had a complementary liability in a new invention of nature—death. And because nature needed a biological limiting factor, "all two-sexed creatures die."

At some point, writes Wylie, ape became non-ape. Man emerged and saw himself "far superior to the rest." Why? What is it, Wylie asks, that differentiates man from other animals, particularly the ape? Answering his own question, he considers such characteristics as animal abilities to speak, reason, and make tools, and, after concluding that these are not essential differences, Wylie claims that all of these traits are products of animal instinct. Even those with the smallest understanding of biology agree with this. But Wylie goes on, they draw the line at man. Man just cannot apply the laws of nature to himself, so he resorts to self-deception.

Opposing the "Christian myth" of an absolute difference between man and animal, Wylie professes that man "emerged gradually; but instinct remained. Man merely hid the fact of it, to enhance the illusion of his own transcendence." His imaginative capabilities allowed him to do so. Because man became aware, because man was confronted with awareness of himself in time, because he could perceive past and future time, a new dimension became accessible and allowed him to believe that he was different from his fellow beasts. Man became inventive and thoughtful, but with this thought came knowledge of death. This was unbearable for man, so he created the belief that death is not really an end, but merely a transference to an afterlife. This concept, an afterlife, allowed man to corrupt the entire schema of nature.

An afterlife implies reward or punishment for good and evil. This implies something other than an instinctual basis for morality. Choice becomes important. Until man corrupted it, wrote Wylie, "all instinct was moral, determining right and wrong perfectly for every species." When man instituted a noninstinctual basis for morality, he turned away from the natural meaning of existence—survival. This, concludes Wylie, was the "beginning of man's perpetual cycle of calamity, his failure to this hour to *be*, as being is meant. . . ." Because man was vain and afraid of death, he perverted the meaning of life, and "he does so still, Christian or pagan, atheist, humanist, or communist." Wylie concludes that man's last hope is to understand the truth about his species and "invent or elicit or discover the 'myth' that best fits our reality as human creatures."

Since man is an animal ruled by instincts, he is also subject to certain instinctual laws. Wylie couples Robert Ardrey's *Territorial Imperative* with Konrad Lorenz's *On Aggression*, and concludes that man is not only subject to the animal dictates of territoriality, but also creates a territorial mental dreamland of faith and religion, which he then protects against intrusion. This hypothesis, as Keefer points out, finally explained to Wylie's own satisfaction why men dogmatically grasp onto their beliefs, killing and sometimes dying for them.

The rest of *The Magic Animal* rambles on, subordinating everything from existentialism to the problems with young Americans to television to the thesis that man has perverted his instinctual programming and thus endangered the very existence of the species. Wylie's main thrust is the excoriation of religion. "Doom," writes Wylie, "has often come fortuitously to individuals and groups. But the doom of nations has generally been mere payment for dishonesty and dishonor, the price for false beliefs and false assumptions, finally collected." What's more, "it is the law of nature that no species, no group and no nation shall misjudge its own nature, or the purposes of that essence without penalty of a like degree, that is, extinction."

The Magic Animal is a tirade against humanists in general. Wylie's main criticism is once again leveled against man's self-deception. Instead of living as nature had intended, man "has buried his natural instinct under phony shibboleths such as religion, capitalism, communism, belief in progress, and blind faith in science." Although Wylie aims his cannon at all things within range, especially religion and materialism, he does posit some position solutions: conservation of resources and ecology.

Man, ignoring his animal nature, has also felt that he can ignore the delicate balance of his natural environment. Wylie believed that this flouting of nature's authority would be man's death blow. He saw that obvious social, moral, and psychological problems had already appeared, and believed that, unless man could harness his own self-destructiveness, the end of the dream would be in short order. Although several critics believed this book to contain some vestige of hope for mankind, it was the beginning of Wylie's pessimistic vision. In *The Magic Animal*, he warned that the earth would soon become uninhabitable if mankind continued to despoil her. By 1971, Wylie's fiction would pessimistically demonstrate that, in his opinion, man had gone too far.

Postscript: Fiction in the Forties

While *Generation of Vipers* and *An Essay on Morals* were Wylie's most notable works in the Forties, he also wrote several serialized and book-length novels. *The Other Horseman* (1941) was a propagandistic series of arguments about American isolationism and the worldwide threat of Fascism. Written prior to Pearl Harbor, the book, like the legendary "other horseman." warned of things to come and was ignored. Its late publication limited its impact, and, as one critic points out, "dulled the edge of its emphasis." The book is not good fiction. Characterization is weak, and the plot is completely subordinated to Wylie's apocalyptic warnings.

The detective story, *Corpses at Indian Stones* (1943), is minor Wylie at best, but two others are worth mentioning. *Night Unto Night* is a searching, penetrating, and often overphilosophized incursion into the mystical connections between life and death. Published in 1944, it is the fictional companion to *Generation of Vipers*. The characters continually vent Wylie's thoughts and criticisms on morals, war, materialism, religion, and, most pointedly, on death. Wylie asserts that part of the meaning of life is to investigate the meaning of death. According to Wylie, the American preoccupation with material objects is nothing more than an attempt to deny the inevitable. Losing their spiritual center, these Americans tend to self-destruct. This is also true of nations. Drawing on Jungian vernacular, Wylie speculates that peace in the world can be attained only when individuals turn inward in search of peace within themselves. This introversion, which turns away from materialism in favor of spiritual values, is, according to Wylie, the way to gain and hold peace among nations.

Wylie's reasoning is Jungian. Mankind is governed by laws which go beyond time, place, and bodily existence. These laws are part of the orderliness of nature, which, when ignored, reveal themselves in war and other collective disjunctions. The solution, writes Wylie, is a religious one, but individual spiritual quest, not public work. Only in this way can a person reunite himself with primary instinctual laws or the collective unconscious. Believing that life and death are parts of something else, and that this greater aspect is different for each individual, Wylie wrote *Night Unto Night* to demonstrate that consciousness has "a relationship to space and time different from the one momentarily in acceptance among university pedants."

If fiction is storytelling, then *Night Unto Night* is on the borderline. There is some plot structure, action, and conflict, but the most conspicuous element in the novel is character development. Through the lives and monologues of four strongly developed characters, Wylie investigates "the living and their thoughts of death." The story is divided into four sections, each concerned with an incident or discussions of incidents which provoke fear, doubt, and speculation about death. The main personalities include: Ann Gracey, the young widow of a coast guard ensign who, though killed at sea, formlessly returns to utter cryptic messages to his wife; John Galen, biochemist, professor, and businessman, an epileptic who learns he will either be cured or die pitifully within the next two years; Ann's sister, Gail Chapman, who lives with the guilt and fear that she was responsible for the asphyxiation deaths of her husband and child, and attempts to evade these thoughts through promiscuity and debauchery; psychiatrist Johann Altheim; and artist Shawn Mullcup, a nonstop talker who mouths most of Wylie's vitriolic opinions, but stands out in the story because he is a raconteur, creating fantastic fables and metaphorical stories.

The plot structure is subtle, taking the reader through several conflicts, but really setting up situations that allow characters to voice Wylie's thoughts about biochemistry, psychology, metaphysics, aesthetics and morality in general. The characters, wrote one critic, come through their conflicts to the realization that "Life. . .is a barrier against actual existence," with the senses being just "five very small peepholes" into the true reality. In the end, they recognize that "death holds the promise not of extinction, but of an astronomically expanded awareness and a transcendent art."

Night Unto Night represents a fleeting moment in Wylie's theory, taking the Jungian idea of racial awareness or collective unconsciousness to a literal extreme. Nevertheless, it is work that shows Wylie in a transitional period. Shawn Mullcup's fables, inserted by Wylie as stories within the overall story, are forerunners to later allegories such as *The Answer* and *The Disappearance*. The inclusion of a treatise by the philosopher-authority, William Percival Gaunt (who reappears in several future novels to voice Wylie's opinions), is another forerunner. Editorializing through fictional treatises is found in much of Wylie's later work, and replaces the direct narrative address of the earlier work. *Night Unto Night* contains all the elements of a well-made novel, although, in final analysis, it still remains a polemic.

Opus 21 (1949)

Opus 21, the fictional correlate to *An Essay on Morals*, is also a philosophical novel. Similar to *Night Unto Night*, it is quasi-fiction, more of a mouthpiece for Wylie's ideas than a bona fide story. It also strongly delineates Freudian and Jungian psychology, not only propounding theories, but actually giving psychoanalytical advice on everything from sexual repression to faulty attitudes on man's biological nature. Jung, as one might expect, plays a major role in the ensuing discussions.

This first-person narration follows the fictional character Philip Wylie (not to be confused with the real Philip Wylie) through one of the most contrived plot structures in the history of literature. Wylie discovers on Thursday that he probably has throat cancer, but by Monday learns that he does not. The novel follows the events that occur in the interim. After learning of his possible doom, Wylie moves into a New York hotel for a week-end of writing. Here he meets Yvonne, a woman who has left her husband because she caught him committing homosexual acts. Yvonne, observes Wylie, is sexually repressed, and her own frigidity is what sent her husband to another man. So, by introducing her to a prostitute, and encouraging her to have a lesbian encounter, he cures her problem. She and her husband live happily ever after. Other unlikely occurrences during this weekend include Wylie's nephew, a nuclear physicist, falling in love with Macia, a whore who is ostensibly reformed but is actually a nymphomaniac; the near seduc-tion of Wylie by three women in three separate incidents; and the near suicide of the nephew after the whore leaves him. The weekend ends with Wylie's discovery that the tumor in his throat is not cancer but a "rare lymphatic growth." This, one critic pointed out, "is a rough weekend for a man who thinks he is dying."

The book is fast moving, reads quickly, but fails on both literary and philosophical levels. The quasi-story contains too much philosophy and psychological advice. This layman's advice, lamented Diana Trilling, "will be the whole lesson the casual reader will draw from the book." Once again, moaned another critic, Wylie is preaching a misinterpreted and amended gospel of Jungian salvation.

The two fables are the high points of the story. The first projects what would happen if, suddenly and unexplainably, cloud formations formed obscene words in the sky. The second fable posits Christ (called Chris) aboard the *Enola Gay* as it was traveling to deliver the first atom bomb to Japan. Both fables force the reader to think and make value judgments. Unfortunately, the rest of the book does not. It presents arguments that fall short of logical soundness and often becomes "a grab bag for the opinions of its unpleasant and neurotic hero," who at times might qualify "as one of the most pretentious bores in all fiction."

CHAPTER IV:
The Atomic Age

World War II represented the breakdown of the authority of law and the standards of morality which mankind had long taken for granted. Heinous crimes and brutality revealed a side of humanity that would forever discredit belief in human dignity and the enlightenment of reason. The war left the world stunned: the past seemed to have been a mistake, and without a more promising set of guidelines, the future was difficult to comprehend, let alone face. The juxtaposition of man's highest capabilities and his lowest bestiality in the explosion of the atomic bomb threw a puzzling and horrifying new light on the perennial question "Who is man?" One histo-rian, Roland Stromberg, wrote: "What the atomic age meant no one could foresee—whether the passing of the human race or its ascent to incom-parably higher levels of material civilization."

On a world level, the atomic age implied a power structure in which the strength of nations would be determined by their nuclear might. On a personal level, it implied the contingency of life. While civilizations had lived with threats of famine and disease, never before was the power of destruction in the hands of man, who might at any minute use it, destroying all that he had hitherto achieved. Atomic power, in itself, could deliver man from the domination of nature but, in the hands of man, could just as easily spell out doom.

Deliverance or Doom

Philip Wylie believed atomic energy to be the hope and the horror of mankind. He had envisioned the coming of the atomic age as early as 1932. Splitting the atom had created the power source for the escape to Bronson Beta in *When Worlds Collide*; it had also created the weaponry for survival. This dichotomy, deliverance or doom, would characterize Wylie's writings through the early Sixties. Then, with the emergence of the nuclear age and the Russian multimegaton nuclear tests, he resigned himself to doom.

While most Americans recoiled in horror at the destruction unleashed by atomic bombs dropped on Hiroshima and Nagasaki, Wylie, knowledgeable about this new power source since his work at the California Institute of Technology in 1930, recognized the emergence of a new age. He had associated with scientists who were optimistic about the future of mankind, and who believed that atomic energy and other advances made by science during the war could now be used for civilian purposes. An almost unlimited potential was envisioned for the future, and Wylie was urging his countrymen to prepare for it.

He believed that atomic energy was only incidentally a military weapon. In articles written in the mid-Forties, he stated that the real potential for atomic energy lay in its use as a power source. This application, he warned, must be made available as quickly as possible, and the future must be planned accordingly. In spite of the fears of potential abuse, atomic energy, he reasoned, is here to stay, with every nation capable of using it against the next. Decency was no longer an issue. "America," wrote Wylie, is a decent nation—and America used the atomic bomb." Power source or weapon, atomic energy would define the future. And Wylie's fiction was, and had been, demonstrating this.

As early as 1939, he had written a story about the Germans making plutonium bombs in a cave in Colorado. "The Paradise Crater," written for *American Magazine*, was, as Sam Moskowitz points out, rejected as "too fantastic," but later was accepted by *Bluebook*, which turned the magazine over to Washington for approval. When Washington balked, the editor of *Bluebook* returned the manuscript to Harold Ober, Wylie's agent, who had "already been contacted by the CIA." Wylie, who had been put under house arrest, was told by an aggressive major that he [the major] would take Wylie's life if necessary, to plug the leak. Wylie agreed to tear up the manuscript, but the decision was made to hold back publication instead. According to Moskowitz, "Four months later, the Atom Bomb was dropped on Hiroshima and *Bluebook* asked to have the story back. It was published in the October, 1945 number." Wylie, through his own research, had learned enough about atomic weaponry to become a security risk [John W.

Campbell, Jr., editor of *Astounding Science Fiction*, went through a similar experience when one of his authors submitted a story featuring an atomic bomb].

But he continued to write stories, many of which exploited the possibilities of atomic disaster. "Blunder," appearing on January 12, 1946, "tells how the world blew itself apart by an atomic accident out of ignorance of simple experimental data" (EoI, p.293). "Philadelphia Phase," written in 1950 for *Colliers*, developed an unlikely situation of the "Americans and Russians co-operating to clean up the rubble of an atomic-bombed city" (EoI, p.294). Of three stories first published by the *Saturday Evening Post* and later combined in book form as *Three To Be Read*, one, "The Smuggled Atom Bomb," adventurously follows Duffer Bogan as he tries to foil a Russian attempt to smuggle atom bomb parts into the United States, and thereby blow up New York. The belief that rocketry and air power were not the only means of delivering an atomic punch would be demonstrated in almost all of Wylie's atomic destruction fiction.

Although atomic weaponry and warfare was his most engaging subject in the Fifties and Sixties, during this time Wylie also produced an even more diversified array of work than he had in the Thirties and Forties. The point here is not to list all or most of Wylie's published work, but rather to point out his astonishing flexibility. Showing the true colors of a free-lance writer, he wrote: "How To Admire Writers" (*Atlantic*, 1950), "Medievalism and the MacArthurian Legend" (*Quarterly Journal of Speech*, 1951), "The Mysterious Doctors of Bimini" (*Saturday Evening Post*, 1954), "The Crime of Mickey Spillane" (*Good Housekeeping*, 1955), "We Are Making a Circus of Death" (*Coronet*, 1950). Wylie, admitting to no limitations, earned a handsome income from these pieces.

Ideas from his magazine articles and journal inclusions often reappeared in Wylie's fiction. Challenged repeatedly as a woman hater, Wylie, when asked by *American Scholar* to respond to several feminist arguments, wrote "Liberty and the Ladies." Here he attempts to expand and clarify the points made in *Generation of Vipers*, which had left him a prime target for feminist writers. His reputation for being a woman hater puzzled him; *Vipers* contained only nineteen pages about "mom" and "Cinderella" and three hundred pages about the "homicidal foibles of men."

Women, writes Wylie, must stop acting like spoiled children and start taking some of the blame for the hideous prospects of the second half of the twentieth century. They are no more or less responsible than the men. Humanity, he writes, is made up of men and women, and the predicament of the twentieth century came about because humanity ignored basic biological-ethical facts. First, a human being is a man plus a woman, an androgynous whole. Second, human beings are animals and their morality should be made compatible with instinct. As far as the battle of the sexes goes, the only method for progress is cooperation, not division and competition. The sexes, he continues, must learn the essence of their complementary differences in nature, those that were intended not only for continuation of the species, but also for pleasure, contentment, understanding, and love.

Concluding "Liberty and the Ladies" with an appeal for an end to the cold war between the sexes, Wylie asserts that concealing or obscuring these differences, or using them combatively, will effectively exterminate the human personality. In his next novel, *The Disappearance*, he attempted to make the point that "love needs a renaissance" through the use of allegory and fantastic fiction; Wylie, in this well-known fiction, took the psychological separation of the sexes to its extreme conclusion.

The Disappearance (1951)

Whether this strangely disturbing tale is science fiction, fantasy, allegory, or a combination of all three, is hard to tell. What is certain is that it departs from precedent and stands as a science fiction classic.

A sudden wresting away of one sex from the other provides the setting for this relentless tirade against American attitudes. When, without reason or explanation, "the females of the species vanished on the afternoon of the second Tuesday in February at four minutes and fifty-two seconds past four o'clock, Eastern Standard Time," Dr. William Percival Gaunt, like the rest of the men in the world, is baffled by the curious event. Likewise, Paula Gaunt, while working in her garden, gazes up to smile at her husband, and right before her eyes—he disappears. So begins the fantastic fable of how the sexes were abruptly separated into two parallel worlds.

In *The Disappearance*, originally written in 1951 and reprinted in 1978, Wylie once again takes on the gadfly role. The tale is a vehicle through which the author expresses his sometimes heavy-handed views on religion, war, science, morality, and, specifically, the idiocies perpetuated by prescribed sexual roles.

The book is two novels within one. It succeeds because Wylie was able to combine an inventive plot with dynamic action and characters who respond believably to four long years of chaos, disaster, and suffering. Dr. William Percival Gaunt, the foremost philosopher of his time, and Paula Gaunt, Ph.D. in foreign languages, wife, and mother, are the leading characters in the story. In separate yet parallel roles, they each help organize and reconstruct their single-sexed worlds. Through their individual struggles and eventual reunion, they illustrate the book's central themes. A "person" is an androgynous construct, and only through the symbiotic functioning of both male and female qualities can human potential be realized. Wylie's use of Jungian theory is even stronger here than in his earlier books, though now the dimension of mysticism is added.

After opening the story with the disappearance itself, Wylie uses flashback techniques to introduce his characters. The Gaunts have had an ordinary life together. He is a well-respected "generalist," and although she is a capable linguist, she is trapped in the limited role of wife and mother. After producing and raising two unimpressive children, they continue to endure the years together. Daughter Edwinna, living with them, embodies the conflicting qualities of beauty, cruelty, and intelligence so often found in Wylie's characters.

The narration of *The Disappearance* is unique. Wylie, concerned with the criticism of his treatment of women in *Generation of Vipers*, takes on the formidable task of alternating chapters from male to female point of view. The technique is effective, allowing for a filling out and exploration of his fantastical premise. If at times Wylie seems to be propagandizing his own ideas too strongly, he does so within the action itself, and therefore does not lose the reader. With the exception of a twenty-four page didactic essay (which is an entire chapter in the text), Wylie is able to infuse the most static situations with movement or the potential for movement.

The plot development personifies the underlying premise of the story. Creative wholeness is only possible in the person who is "a-man-plus-a-woman." With one or the other missing, there can be hate and destruction, but no creativity and love. Wylie, through the book, alternates between male and female worlds, depicting destruction and hardship. The sense of loss and emptiness in each world slowly grows into resentment and hate. Most of the story is the chronicle of humankind's physical and spiritual disintegration. On one level, it depicts two separate worlds disintegrating. On another level, it scolds society for forcing men and women into separate psychological and material domains. The war between the sexes is the result of an unenlightened attitude which overlooks the fundamental truth discussed in "Liberty and the Ladies": there is only one sex, with men and women being halves.

The allegorical stories begin in the male world. The men are taken by surprise when the women physically disappear, unaware that they are already spiritually separate from the women. The immediate aftermath of the disappearance is bewilderment. Although the male-dominated government and business worlds function fairly well, the international reverberations are quite different. Wylie, once again playing upon popular fears, has the Russians take advantage of the disappearance to justify an atomic attack on the Americans, and the intensive three-day atomic war is gruesomely described. While the Americans lose three cities, the Russians lose seventeen, and the war itself. The men revert to primitive, instinctual savagery. The qualities of hate and destruction take over as law and order fail, the men running in packs, killing and looting, turning to homosexuality and female impersonation. Throughout all of this, William Gaunt's committee of scientists, scholars, and philosophers is unable to explain the cause of the disappearance.

The women, in their separate world, are in worse shape than the men. Left to their own resources after the disappearance, the women are unprepared for even the simplest tasks confronting them. They are typical "moms" and "Cinderellas," barely capable of survival because they are wives of politicians rather than politicians, and consumers of products rather than businessmen. Through the organizational skills of some women like Paula and Edwinna Gaunt, a government comprised of congressmen's wives is set up. Sidestepping the possible disaster of atomic war, the American women are plagued with various natural catastrophes and epidemics. Unable to run the sophisticated equipment necessary for mining and unable to operate complicated machinery, they suffer from inadequate food supplies, lack of medical treatment, and a general breakdown of morality. The women soon resent and hate the men who made them so dependent. Again, destructive forces are promulgated by the absence of the other sex.

The sexes are reunited on the fourth anniversary of the disappearance, ironically Valentine's Day. Suddenly, in an instant, the world is restored to the way it was four years earlier. Men and women once again walk the same streets. Loved ones who had died in the separation period are restored to life. People who had spent four hellish years apart begin great and joyous orgies. Without ever understanding why the disappearance occurred, people are back together, understanding now that men and women are one.

In Kafka's *Metamorphosis*, the main character, Gregor, is so dehumanized in life that he actually wakes up one morning to find himself transformed into an enormous cockroach. In Wylie's *The Disappearance*, the men and women are so separated from their own vital male and female qualities that they actually disappear into separate worlds. Unlike Kafka, Wylie gives his characters a second chance. When the men and women are rejoined, and given a moment to reflect, they realize that it is only through male and female energies that the creative forces of the universe work. Men and women are equal parts of life's creative wholeness, separate and different only in their individual functions.

Wylie, in this allegorical fable, uses different metaphors than he did in his earlier work. The appeal to a personal God is gone. There are no images of the familiar old man sitting on his throne in judgment. There is, rather, the allusion to a creative principle or force that is universally present in the collective unconscious. The author's continued use of archetypal concepts and symbolism indicates his adherence to Jungian ideas.

The closest explanation for the disappearance itself is couched in Jungian terms. An obscure character in the story, cryptically at work building a mandala-shaped room in his house, suddenly begins to have vivid and accurate dreams of the women in their separate world. He does not know why he builds the structure, only that he is compelled to do so. Nevertheless, the room brings him into contact with the instinctual basis of the species, the unified collective unconscious; and he is momentarily able to transcend the separateness. There is a fire: the room is destroyed; the dreams stop; the story continues.

The Disappearance will be stimulating to some and disquieting to others. There is, of course, the Wyliean sideshow of atomic warfare and its aftermath of rioting and rebellion in the male world. There is natural calamity and disease in the female world. These opportunities for projected horror had been present in Wylie's earliest work and would be even stronger in his next novel. But *The Disappearance* represents a change in Wylie's writing. It is less vitriolic than his earlier work and more subdued than some of his later work. But it most notably shows an amelioration in his position about women. Yet, even with his explicitly nonsexist premise, he would continue to be known as the man who hated women.

Although civil defense became one of his major concerns in the Fifties and Sixties, Wylie, as early as the mid-Forties, had formulated plans for early control and regulation of atomic energy. Among other suggestions, he recommended that science be internationalized, that scientists be brought into the mainstream of government, that an international advisory committee of scientists be formed for the planet, that the secrets of atomic energy be made public, and that atomic energy, as an industry, be nationalized. This plan, naive as it might be, is the best example of Wylie's early optimistic belief that Americans were responsible for dealing with this new "atomic present in a rational and intensely helpful way."

This "dream" of American civility and responsibility in the atomic age would dissipate quickly as cold war tensions multiplied and the paranoia of the Fifties set in. While he had written earlier of American science promising "a paradise men can make with their hands and their own minds," Wylie quickly changed his posture. Now believing that atomic power was closer to doom than deliverance, he began writing articles, and ultimately a book, about civil defense and defense preparations. "A Better Way to Beat the Bomb," written in 1951 for *Atlantic*, argued for a reassessment of civil defense programs. Representing a definite change in the author's thinking, this article noted ineffectual planning, political irresponsibility, and lack of vision in the American civil defense programs. America, reasoned Wylie, never had the chance to test its CD programs, and in spite of the traditional American courage, citizens would be led to slaughter if the poorly conceived evacuation plans were ever evoked. Decentralization, "ribbon cities," and World War II "local" civil defense units were inadequate to handle attacks by the advanced weaponry which would be created.

Evacuating cities in wartime also appalled Wylie. His sense of patriotism and courage was offended by such "cowardice." Furthermore, it wasn't American. If a war is to be won, he reasoned, someone had to run the vital cities, even if those cities were under attack. True, the traditional precautionary means must be taken, but more importantly, experts must be organized and mobilized to go swiftly to any attacked area. Localities must have coordinated efforts for "interlocked and mutual missions" of aid and rescue. From Day One, wrote Wylie, all citizens would be front line warriors, and an alert, well-informed citizenry must be backed up by a nation capable of responding to an enemy attack.

Tomorrow! (1953)

After four years as a consultant to the Federal Civil Defense Administration, Wylie wrote *Tomorrow!*, his first novel specifically about atomic warfare. Disenchanted with the "official position" on civil defense, Wylie, who had already written several instructive articles on the subject, believed that the public needed concrete illustrations in order to understand the possible devastating results of atomic bombs. In "Safe and Insane," written for *Atlantic* in 1949, he asserted that the uninformed public, already predisposed to national hysteria, would be psychologically devastated by atomic destruction, unless they were graphically introduced to the reality of it. *Tomorrow!* did both. Half of it is a debate for national preparedness through civil defense. The second half portrays the reality of atomic devastation, vividly describing the physical aftermath, and, for all purposes, proving Wylie's points about civil defense.

Dedicated to the "gallant men and women of the Federal Civil Defense Administration and to those other true patriots, the volunteers, who are doing their best to save the sum of things," the book is admittedly rigged to demonstrate that the official position on how the American people would respond in an attack was wrong. "They aren't ready for it," pointed out Wylie in an interview in 1954. He believed that few people were capable of thinking with detachment and intelligence. And since most were not, he wanted this book to be the *Uncle Tom's Cabin* of the atomic age.

Tomorrow! was originally written as a scenario for the movies, aiming at the cinema's massive audience. Wylie, according to interviewer Lewis Nichols, tried in vain to peddle the screenplay; but because film makers were afraid of the expense, Wylie, a couple of years later, turned the scenario into a novel. The author's hope that "everyone in the country" would become familiar with the facts of atomic warfare was nearly accomplished. The book reached the best seller list and a substantial number of readers, and it created quite a national stir.

The story details an atomic attack on two neighboring cities in mid-America. It is a presentation of opposites, revealing polar positions not only on civil defense but on values American. In this sense, *Tomorrow!* is a typical Wylie novel, but with a twist. As one critic pointed out, "the heroes and heroines of *Tomorrow!* are much the same as in previous polemics. But where formerly they cried for a decrease in sexual pretense, they are now clamoring for an increase in civil defense."

The Conner family, living in Green Prairee, where civil defense systems are a model of efficiency, are the new Wylie ideal. Father Henry is a civil defense sector warden, a bastion of strength, middle class virtue, and enlightenment. Mother Beth, daughter Nora, and sons Ted and Charles all combine to form the ideal civil defense-oriented family. The Bailey family, also living in Green Prairee, shun civil defense and lead lives of capitalistic greed and social visibility. The two families are contrasted throughout the book, though joined together by a romance between the Conner son, Chuck, and the Bailey daughter, Lenore, who has been "persuaded" by her family to marry a wealthy, yet empty-headed, shallow young man. The human conflicts are typically Wylie, with love triangles and middle-class hypocrisy continually surfacing. The rest of the characters in the story are taken from the Conner-Bailey mold, each representing the stereotypical middle-class American and each taking on an aspect of Wylie's *Generation of Vipers* vision.

River City is located on the other side of Green Prairie River, and its citizens demonstrate the "it can't happen here" attitude, as far as civil defense is concerned. It represents the common American attitude, and ultimately suffers for this arrogance. Wylie delves into personal lives here, also, with most characters again created as various standard Wyliean types.

Condition Yellow becomes Condition Red on December 23, 1961, as the nation's cities are filled with last minute Christmas shoppers, and civil defense outfits are scattered and unprepared. When the bombs begin to fall, the characters show their true colors. The prepared citizens of Green Prairee are valiant and cool, while the unprepared in Green Prairee and the entire

48

population of River City become uncontrollable, panic-stricken mobs. Bombs destroy New York, Washington, Detroit, and Philadelphia. Twenty-five cities are attacked, including Green Prairee and River City, killing some twenty million people through the combination of bombs, fire, germ warfare, and general panic.

The description of atomic death and domestic havoc is the most striking aspect of the book. Children are mangled by shattered glass, people are roasted alive, faces burned into unrecognizable blobs, and, perhaps, most frighteningly a man, caught by surprise in the attack, flees through the streets on the stubs of his ankle-bones, his feet severed by the blast! The descriptions continue, each more horrible than the last, each destined to reappear in the reader's dreams. In a word, the good, civil defense-minded people are spared, and the bad, unprepared people are brutally killed.

Ultimately, though, the President is killed and another put in his place, and the issue becomes one of surrendering to the Russian ultimatum or sticking it out. Because no true Wyliean American would think of surrendering, the sparsely-populated congress decides to use the "secret weapon"—the largest hydrogen bomb ever assembled. The bomb is launched from a submarine, *The Nautilus*, and the tables are quickly turned. Wylie describes the result of the bomb's explosion: "The rays, the temperatures, vaporized Finland's gulf in a split part of an instant. The sea's bottom was melted. The light reached out into the universe. Finland was not. Lithuania, Latvia, Esthonia, they were not. Kronstadt melted, Leningrad. The blast kicked up the ashes that once had been Moscow, collecting the burning environs and pulverized them and hurled their dust at the Urals. . .The last war was finished."

The world is largely in ruin, but saved from the communist peril. River City is destroyed. Green Prairee lives. The personal conflicts, many of which continue throughout the story, are solved with the central romance between Lenore Bailey and Chuck Conner. The two marry and live happily ever after. Like *The Disappearance*, this book ends romantically. The ruined world is to be rebuilt by those who can better design not only the cities but also general values. There is hope for the future, as Henry Conner, responding to the question of why River City faired so badly while Green Prairee came through the attack relatively unscathed, states: "Hell, time we quite talking about it! Only difference was, some of us tried to swap freedom for security; the rest of us went on fighting for freedom, as usual."

There is no question that *Tomorrow!* was propagandistic. Wylie's objective was to waken "a sleepwalking nation," and the public awoke. The critics, also awakened, were more rancorous than the public at large, who were already panic-stricken about the atomic bomb anyway. One critic wrote that it is undoubtedly good that Wylie got these feelings off his chest, but "at the risk of being unpatriotic," it can be noted that "the book should not be confused in any way with the novel as an art form, or with literature at all." Others concurred. Many objected to the "soap opera" quality of the story and the author's presumptuous 4000-word editorial on civil defense, uttered through the persona of one of the characters in the middle of the story.

Other objections to this novel can also be made. Clearly, it is didactic. The characters are often reduced to mouthpieces for the author. The personal traumas and petty romances are contrived, and, more often than not, unrealistically portrayed. As H. H. Holmes [Anthony Boucher], critic for the *New York Herald Tribune* wrote, "It is hard to believe that the author of *The Disappearance* could, even under the pressure of more than his normal quota of indignation, have produced so shallow a work of fiction." But Irwin Clark saw the author's point more clearly. He points out the book may be in the form of the novel, but really isn't—or shouldn't be considered as—one. "The point of the book," he goes on, "is to impress the reader with the horrible destructiveness of such an attack, and with the almost equally great horrors which the unprepared and undisciplined hordes of civilians will inflict upon themselves in the ensuing mad panic."

Although not impressed by the book, the critic for *Time* correctly points out that the best parts of *Tomorrow!* "are Wylie's orgiastic descriptions of falling bombs and U. S. cities going up in sky-high sheets of fire." He goes on: "Wylie has been expecting a large scale annihilation of his erring fellow men for many years and can therefore write of it with passionate intensity." Unfortunately, the passionate intensity to warn Americans of the dangers of being unprepared was short-lived. *Tomorrow!*, writes Sam Moskowitz, "was outdated within six months of its publication in 1954; the development of fusion weaponry destroyed its validity" (EoI, p.294-295). Truman Keefer agrees, pointing out that the book had little chance to change public attitudes or government procedures.

Wylie, now less interested in civil defense, which could only provide protection from atomic weaponry, concerned himself with those devices which might prevent a war, the only real way to deal with nuclear weaponry. He considered the prospect of disarmament, but realized that, before this step could be taken, the public must be made aware that two oft-stated premises were illusions. Contrary to general belief, victory is not possible in a nuclear war. Therefore, war, in a nuclear age, is not an acceptable arbitrating force in world affairs. In order to dramatize what would happen if nuclear war were brought home to the United States, and demonstrate the full meaning of modern armaments, Wylie now spent much of his energy writing either horrifyingly graphic descriptions of the potential holocaust, or allegorical fables which demonstrated the folly of man acting as God. Mankind's only hope lay in avoidance of confrontation, not confrontation itself.

The Answer (1954)

Nowhere is Wylie more of a prophet than in his short novelette, *The Answer*, which first appeared in *Saturday Evening Post*, and was subsequently issued in book form. In *The Disappearance* he physically separated the sexes for four long years because they had lost sight of their own instinctual natures. In *Tomorrow!* he vaporized half of the world because the people had been irrational in handling atomic power and in preparing for atomic war. But in *The Answer* the consequences of scientific research gone astray and mankind's disregard for the basic qualifications of love and compassion are far more poetic. Here Wylie speaks for truth above dogma, pleading through metaphor with the scientist, theologian, and statesman for rationality in the nuclear age.

The Answer proved to be one of Wylie's most popular stories, making him "the oracle of the atomic age." This simple tale builds on one imaginative incident: the accidental killing of two angels—one by America and the other by Russia—during experimental H-bomb tests. The story opens as Major General Marcus Scott, a man more literary than military, is pacing the deck of the *USS Ticonderoga*, nervously awaiting the results of an H-bomb detonation. For some reason, Scott is uneasy and sad, and has the feeling of impending failure, as if "we will finally manage to produce a dud." Nevertheless, the blast occurs. "Slowly the sky blew up. . .the thing swelled and swelled and rose. . .the fireball burned within itself and around itself, burnt the sea away—a hole in it—and a hole in the planet—had it been a city, Baltimore—the urban tinder and the people, would have hair-fired in the debris."

Although the test appears to be successful, there is a "casualty," a matter of import Z. Scott, whose sense of mystical wrongness has held true, is informed that a Tempest Island missionary and his son have discovered something peculiar. His investigations leave him speechless: in a glade on the island lies a body: "The beautiful human face slept in death; the alabastrine body was relaxed in death; the unimaginable eyes were closed; and the immense white wings were folded." There is no question about it— the body is all that remains of an angel.

Scott learns from Ted Simms, the only witness to the accident, that the angel had fallen from the sky like a wounded bird, and upon hitting the ground, sat up, crying to the boy, "I was a little late." Then, after tucking its wings, it died. Keeping the "casualty" a secret, Scott informs the President and has the body sent to the United States on a B-111. The airplane is unexplainably lost at sea. The government is perplexed. Theologians and scientists irrationally maintain their dogmas, each explaining the "casualty" as something other than an angel.

At about the same time, the Russians accidentally wound and kill another angel. The "unfeeling" premier, who is "ruthless by any standard in history," knows that this discovery will finish the "dream of Engels, Marx and the rest" as well as put an end to communism. Hence, he decides to destroy the remains in the nuclear blast scheduled for the next day. There shall be no intervention, he thinks to himself, when the surprise blitz is launched on the USA, "whom we shall slaughter in sudden millions, soon."

Major General Scott returns to Tempest Island at Christmas. Here he sees Ted Simms, the missionary boy who had witnessed the angel's death, and learns that the boy's father has gone mad from the experience. He also learns that the boy had omitted something in the earlier report—the angel had dropped a gold book when falling from the sky. Containing the wisdom of the galaxy, the book is retrieved from beneath the rock where the boy had hidden it. Although a similar book was dropped in the Soviet Union, it "had been reduced to fractions of its atoms by a certain test weapon which had destroyed the body of its bearer." In both, the message is the same.

The answer to mankind's unholy predicament is: "Love one another."

Clearly, this is an allegorical story. It is also propagandistic, not unlike many of Wylie's atomic age stories. Once again, Wylie presents his fundamental philosophy through fiction. Here, the point is taken from *An Essay on Morals*, and it is another demonstration of entrenched dogma versus the "never-ending search for truth." Outside of his outlandish portraits of the Russians, the book deals impartially with nationalistic, scientific, and theological dogma. All dogmatic responses conceal truth and allow for self-deception. "The angels," writes Keefer, "are, in effect, *reality*; and the most important message in the story is not that man can find salvation through loving his fellows; rather the point is that salvation can come only through loving truth, a far more difficult enterprise" (PW, p.130).

This "credo for the nuclear age," as Moskowitz describes it, has been printed in several collections of stories and in single book form. It was, if one is to rely on the blurbs accompanying the story, well received as allegory. Bernard Baruch commented that the story was interesting and beautiful. Eleanor Roosevelt felt that the story "indicates our desire not to destroy and our belief that only a spiritual feeling may move us," while Norman Vincent Peale described the story as "unique and strangely moving." Carl Sandburg, in perhaps the most accurate assessment, compared *The Answer* with *Pilgrim's Progress* or the Four Horsemen of the Apocalypse, and further commented that it "mingles merciless realism with hazardous mysticism." Regardless of the validity of these observations, *The Answer* has become one of the most widely read and remembered of Wylie's shorter fictions. It follows closely the pattern of *The Disappearance*, and in spite of a few glaring errors (How can one "kill" an angel?), it is wonderfully written. It marks the end of the atomic age for Wylie; he henceforth felt that there was no protection against this new nuclear potential.

Triumph (1963)

The other way to dissuade people from the "romantic" notions of war is to graphically demonstrate them through gruesome description. Wylie's second major novel about World War III, *Triumph*, does just that. Financially but not artistically successful, the novel reveals an almost sadistic Philip Wylie, both in the sense of his realism and in his gratuitous brutalization of a public already horrified by the Cold War. But, in all fairness, he needed to popularize and sell books at this point in his career. The late Fifties and early Sixties had been, Truman Keefer points out, a difficult time for Philip Wylie. The years between 1957-1967 were "marked by a serious decline in quality as well as in quantity" of his writing, leading to "a long downward slide of his literary reputation." Financial difficulties, drug and alcohol dependency, and marital difficulties all converged on this normally prolific writer, resulting in "six years passing [prior to *Triumph*] before Wylie was able to produce a publishable work" (PW, p.131,134).

Wylie, looking for the financial return, published *Triumph* in expurgated form in *Saturday Evening Post*, which had agreed to print it if some of the more gruesome sections were removed. The book itself was then issued in its entirety by Doubleday. Although it did achieve financial success, *Triumph* was not up to Wylie's earlier work. It would become a best seller because it scared the public and because it "reworked the most overworked gimmick of our time." Most critics and reviewers agreed that the book was bad, though they knew that it would sell in spite of itself.

The book reads like a soap opera. Set in the Nineteen Seventies, *Triumph* is the story of fourteen survivors of a sneak Soviet thermonuclear attack on America. Dr. Ben C. Bernman, the brilliant department head at Brookline Atomic Research facility, is a weekend guest at Uxmal, the Connecticut estate of Vance Farr, wealthy exporter and Renaissance man, and his alcoholic wife, Valerie. The weekend festivities are interrupted by the civil defense sirens; the servants and guests are rapidly evacuated to Vance Farr's "Panic Palace," an extravagant fallout shelter housed five hundred feet beneath the surface of a limestone quarry. Fourteen carefully chosen characters are confined hereafter in the opulent subterranean sanctuary.

Housed within the earth are the Farrs, their beautiful daughter Faith, who is engaged to playboy Kit Barlow but in love with Bernman, the man responsible for saving her life in an automobile accident. Also present is the Negro butler Paulus Davey and his beautiful Vassar graduate daughter, Connie; a Japanese engineer; a Chinese Radcliffe graduate; a meter reader from the utility company; an exotic dancer; her gigolo boyfriend; and two children aged seven and twelve. The shelter protecting this unlikely group has been sumptuously stocked to support fifteen people for nearly two years. The supplies, far from mere necessity, include the most advanced technological gimmickry and life-support systems, gourmet foods, a library, recreational facilities, and everything else imaginable.

Triumph is several stories within one book. The author comfortably jumps from section to section, approaching each incident from a different perspective. After two expository chapters in which he develops the characters and setting, Wylie, continuing with the third-person narrative throughout, jumps into the action. The President is awakened by the "green" phone. He is informed that a "volunteer" Red army has invaded Yugoslavia. The "Reds" have warned the free world not to interfere lest they destroy London and Paris. The United States has two hours to respond. Although they agree not to attack, the Russians, with characteristic duplicity, launch the suicidal attack. The President is killed but the counter-attack is launched. The Northern hemisphere quickly becomes a lifeless wasteland.

Although the United States, Russia, and China appear to be annihilated, the evil-scheming Russians have clandestinely tucked several thousand people into protected mountain refuges; they emerge after the destruction, intending to take over the remainder of the world. In the end, however, the last remains of the United States Navy launches "Operation Last Ditch," destroying the emerging "ruskies," though not before they themselves are destroyed.

The group below, however, survives (minus one who kills himself). The war, with mechanistically programmed missiles and straggling forces, lasts several years. How the lucky fourteen survive, and how human nature reveals itself during the two-year wait, is, unfortunately, the largest part of this novel. Wylie resorts to diversion, using unrealistic technologies, cheap gimmickry, and a stock of male-macho incidents. He should have avoided the human melodrama and focused instead on the technical description he was so good at. As it turns out, even the technical description lacks credibility, and is, in many spots, unreadable.

The description of the holocaust is gruesome: scenes include melting eyes, bodies torn in half, babies ambling blindly with entrails dangling (and pulled out by each crawling movement forward!). Wylie took great pains to describe accurately the ecological effects of the nuclear devices, with much of his civil defense experience and knowledge of advanced weaponry revealing itself.

The resolution is unsatisfactory. When the survivors are rescued by an Australian mercy mission, the reader feels that the author was too tired to finish the book, opting for the quickest ending possible. After allowing oneself to be bored by the antics of these surviving oddities, sickened by the descriptions of death and destruction, and frightened by the actual thought of nuclear destruction, this underdeveloped conclusion is a disappointment.

The critics were almost unanimous. The fourteen survivors of this nuclear mess, wrote one critic, were "assembled by means as bizarre as their own personalities." He goes on: Their "two years underground constitutes one of the wasted opportunities of modern fiction," concluding with a suspenseful but unsatisfying resolution. Another critic pointed out that "we need shelters against the fallout of gimmick literature which rains down on us." Wylie, wrote another, "wants to say something about the sickness of our society, but, ironically, his new novel is itself a symptom of the sickness."

By the mid-Sixties, Americans were more readily questioning the science, technology, urbanization, and corporate growth that had become almost a religion in the Forties and Fifties. It did not take long before science itself became overwhelming, "and for the first time since the emergence of modern science, men felt themselves unable to control what they had discovered. Technology was often dehumanizing, transferring the center of gravity from the individual to the machine." People, by 1965, were beginning to realize that technology, continuing at an increasingly rapid rate, could alienate them from their fellow man. A period of anger and social upheaval was approaching, perhaps as a backlash for all of the years of nuclear fear and frustration. Wylie too, by 1965, had grown tired of warning humanity about nuclear disaster.

They Both Were Naked, published by Doubleday in 1965, was a departure from Wylie's disaster fiction and a return to the polemical format of his earlier novels. Written in first-person narrative and once again featuring the fictional writer, Philip Wylie, the story is another investigation into contemporary manners and morals. This time the target is big business. Fictional Wylie has been commissioned to write a biography of D. Luder Phyfe and his industrial empire, but soon learns of the financier's unsavory affairs in life and business, which include various sexual, business, and even incestual indiscretions.

This poorly conceived and badly written book is over-philosophical and prolix. It becomes painfully boring after Wylie (the author) begins detailing the actions of Wylie (the character). The story stops and starts like a badly tuned automobile, and Wylie's discussions and indictments of American values and morality obscure the plot, story, and even the characters, who are ill-defined even at story's end. His opinions are inexhaustible and irrepressible, and although their expression worked for him throughout his career, in *Naked* these heavy-handed opinions force the reader to close the book. "Perhaps it is time," concluded one critic, "that a kindly cop asked him gently to move along."

Wylie moved along into a new genre with *The Spy Who Spoke Porpoise*. This entrance into espionage, agents, and counteragents was, according to Keefer, written merely for the author's own amusement, not to please his publishers or the public. In fact, it had little chance to please anyone, because it was poorly promoted and sold by Doubleday, its publisher (PW, p.146). Written in 1969, the book tells the story of R. Grove, an ex-OSS officer who, after discovering certain clandestine affairs in the U. S. intelligence service, is secretly commissioned by the President as a spy to thwart both internal and external threats to national security. Grove, similar to James Bond in ability and Matt Helm in gruffness, is a strong machismo figure, yet highly intelligent and sensitive. He does less direct philosophizing than other Wylie characters, though his inner thoughts do so indirectly. In all, this is a story that is both exciting and soundly constructed. By the end of the Sixties, modern science, religion, and philosophy had, it seemed, all conspired to dispel the certainty of meaning and purpose in man's finite world. Man, as the Seventies began, would once again be forced to question his very being, his inherent significance, and his apparently malfunctioning values. Wylie, as the decade turned over, had been growing more and more pessimistic about the future of man. Almost twenty-five years after *Generation of Vipers*, the world had still not heeded his warnings. Like the legendary "other horseman," he was now not only ignored, but reviled and ridiculed. Still expounding the view that man was destroying the world that he lived in, Wylie, in 1970, would have a heart attack that would leave him bedridden. He would die the following year, but not before he took on America's rebellious youth, whom he considered the new generation of Vipers, and the spoilers of the earth, whom he considered mankind's most dangerous enemies.

CHAPTER V:
The End of the Dream

The violence and political dissent of the Sixties contrasted sharply with the placidity of the previous decade. Opening with the election of John F. Kennedy, moving tragically forward with the quiet ascension of Lyndon B. Johnson, and corruptly ending with the presidency of Richard M. Nixon, the decade of the Sixties saw major political, social, and economic changes on the American front. The Civil Rights movement, ghetto rioting, three assassinations, anti-war activities, student disorders, the shutting down of Harvard, Columbia, and Cornell, the invasion of Cambodia, and the shooting deaths of four students at Kent State University all occurred in this ten-year span. The radicalism manifest in American youth by 1970 represented a new political awareness.

Out of this awareness came a direct challenge to the American values of the previous decades. George Babbitt was now an anachronism, and Zenith City, with all its glitter and pseudo-values, was aflame. The rallying cry of American youth was "power to the people," and their feeling of social responsibility took precedence over the drive for social affluence. The organization man, conformity, bomb shelters, and materialism were out; dropping out, nonconformity, pacifism, and spiritual values were in. With the political goals of the new left and the social goals of ethical reformists, most of Philip Wylie's early social criticism was being implemented.

The Sons and Daughters of Mom (1971)

Theoretically, of course, Wylie should have applauded the efforts of youth. But he didn't. He was minimally involved, spoke on a few campuses, but was no supporter of the youth revolution, which he saw as "idiotic." Instead, with the compulsion to write so strong that he "interrupted another effort, a work of fiction long in gestation, to do so," he wrote another polemic. *Sons and Daughters of Mom*, the result of his compulsion, is a fire and brimstone tirade "about the Under-Thirties, the New People, the Revolutionaries and Rebels, the Activists and the Blacks, the New Left, the Hippies, the Cop-Outs and Dropouts, their Drug Scene, their Sex Revolution, their Reasonable Rage and Unreasonable, their Confrontations, Protests, Nonnegotiable Demands, and strict Conventions."

Having already made "every criticism and criminal charge that young America" was then making, Wylie believed that he could relate to the children of those he had attacked a quarter of a century earlier. He really couldn't, and they weren't interested. The book, written in typical Wyliean hyperbole, failed both as rhetoric and as philosophy, and failed to make even the smallest impact on the public. It deserved to fail. Filled with unqualified generalizations and obvious oversimplifications and misunderstandings, the book appeared to be written by a cranky old man, a "curmudgeon," as Melvin Maddox, of the *Christian Science Monitor*, described him.

In eighteen repetitive chapters, Wylie acts as an intercessor between the parties to the generation gap, explaining to each side "what neither had or has, to exchange." Beginning with an embarrassingly literal-minded response to youth's generalization about those over thirty, Wylie states: "Nothing whatever *happens* to any person, let alone to all, on a thirtieth birthday. Even as a symbol, the number has had no meaning. How could it apply to one who did not know his or her date of birth?" The book goes downhill from there.

It continues with an attack on his old target, the Liberal Intellectual Establishment (LIE), who, "like the student rebels, consider themselves as an elite." These Puddingheads, wrote Wylie, have been mistaken in "every major view for the past half century." Wylie then blasts higher education, which "was designed in the dark ages by monks to maintain the dark forever," the sins and virtues of materialism, and momism, a reiteration of his earlier attack to show that the whole society has taken on the material-istic orientation once reserved for mom. Other chapters banter with "squares and radicals," American sex roles, the silent majority, blacks, "girl-haired boys," and pot. But few are well argued or even compre-hensible.

After eighteen long chapters, Wylie, in his own words, "quits." Although the book ends on a hopeful note, it is obvious from the writing and from the lack of careful editing and writerly concern that Wylie was an old man, discouraged, nearing the end. This is confirmed by Keefer, who notes that, after a year of writing, rewriting, revising, editing, and redoing the text, Wylie was still struggling. "Never before. . .had he been forced into so much laborious emendation" which "exacted a fearful physical and emotional toll, and the more ill and exhausted he became, the harder the writing was." Wylie, according to Keefer, knew that this would be his last chance to set out his ideas. It completely drained him.

Philosophically, *Sons* falls short of *Generation of Vipers* and exhibits careless logic. It reiterates much of what Wylie said in *The Magic Animal* and provides no real change in position. The world had drastically changed since *Vipers* was written in 1943. Wylie, it appeared, had not. Few would listen to his ranting and raving. Too many people were doing it elsewhere more effectively and more outrageously. It's not so much Mr. Wylie's fault, wrote Melvin Maddox, as the fault of the times. "Nothing seems as black and white as it did twenty-five years ago, and that's bad news for a cur-mudgeon. About the worst thing Mr. Wylie can say against the Young is that they don't know what they're for. The worst one can say about Mr. Wylie is that he no longer knows what he is against." Criticizing everything from television to mystical religions, Wylie now appeared more confused than angry, a quality that hitherto had not been found in his writing.

Wylie's final two works reflect his disillusionment and despair about the future of mankind. For nearly one-half of a century, he had excoriated his fellow man, warning him to reconsider his irrational behavior before it was too late. In his earliest writing, he warned against anachronistic morali-ty, sexual repression, unthinking dogma, and self-deception. In his middle years, he warned against irrational civil defense planning and the threat of atomic disaster. In his final years, he warned against abusing the planet and flouting nature's authority.

Actually, Wylie had always been aware of the need for environmental controls. He had been close to nature as a young boy, had become a boy scout by the time he was fourteen, and was capable of putting most flowers and plants into their botanical categories by the time he was nineteen. In fact, much of his theory of the importance of instinct grew out of his early observation of animals in their natural habitat. Later, in his earliest novels and stories, his characters indirectly revealed themselves through their attitudes toward their natural surroundings. Hugo Danner, for example, was not only a product of man's tampering with nature, but revealed a certain reverence toward the forces around him. In the end, it is nature, a lightning bolt, which frees him from his torment. Obviously, stories such as *When Worlds Collide*, *The Murderer Invisible*, and *The Savage Gentleman* build around the awesome but lawful forces of nature.

Although known to most Americans as a writer of novels and social criticism, Wylie, in the Forties, was one of four advisors to The Lerner Marine Laboratory in Bimini. There he learned about the delicate balance of ecosystems within the sea, studied algae, learned about small invertebrates, classified the flora on the island and sea plants off the reefs, and developed a great respect for ecology. His passion for and knowledge of fishing, most often revealed in the "Crunch and Des" stories, nurtured an attitude of respect in Wylie for the sublimity of nature.

By the Fifties, Wylie had begun to write about the dangers of chemicalizing food. American food, he points out in "Science Has Spoiled My Supper," might look appetizing, but it has neither taste nor nutritional value. Granted, he saw food processing as another example of the decline of American individualism, but, in this 1954 article, he hypothesizes a later proven fact: Americans are fat and undernourished, in spite of their affluence. The nutritional value of food had been replaced by preservatives, and people ate more because their "instinctual" need to taste and enjoy was not met.

Selfishness and the exercise of privilege, writes Wylie in another article, will destroy Florida unless "the grasping boobs and the merely ignorant despoilers" can be stopped in time. This mild warning from 1956 was, five years later, replaced by another. "We Americans are plainly the greatest nest foulers in history. Most of our streams, rivers, ponds, and lakes are polluted." Our seacoasts, he goes on in "Why Are They Spoiling Florida?" are contaminated, our cities are smothered beneath automobile fumes, and the water supplies are threatened by poor drainage. "The exploitation of natural resources, along with shortsighted or irresponsible planning and bad engineering, are acts of men." "These," he concludes, "are directions—neat and absolute—for suicide."

Wylie's final cause, that of saving the environment, was obviously the culmination of these years of concern. From 1968 to his death in 1971, Wylie tried various means of bringing his message home to the American public. The approach was similar to that taken against America's irrational atomic and nuclear policies. First, in *The Magic Animal*, he tried reason, attempting to educate the public through didactic essays. When this had little effect, he tried scare tactics, attempting to frighten the public into awareness. He wanted large audiences to view the graphic demonstration of environmental consequences, and, while he had failed to find a producer for his movie on atomic destruction, the idea of environmental disaster was ripe for television. "Los Angeles: A.D. 2017" was an episode written for NBC's series, *The Name of the Game*, though, when produced, was "drastically revised, with many of his important details excised." Keefer, who had been interviewing Wylie at the time, comments that "Wylie was furious," and, because he had been given the rights for novelization, "turned out a ninety-thousand word novel that, except in the general outline of the plot, bears little resemblance to the televised version" (PW, p.151).

Los Angeles: A.D. 2017 (1970); *The End of the Dream* (1972)

Both of these books of environmental apocalypse employ the same hard-edged realism. Neither of them has strong plot structure; each is closer to a series of incidents than to a story. While the former is the expression of a specific attitude as well as a story, *The End of the Dream* is merely the expression of mood, which may have resulted from having been compiled and published after Wylie's death in 1971.

Los Angeles: A.D. 2017 portrays the dark and pessimistic future result of man's excessiveness. The mood is one of hopelessness about the future of the planet and man; the tone is bitter, caustic, and cutting. Wylie's descriptions of environmental conditions and disasters are frightening, less of a warning than a statement of fact. Whereas in the past he had warned of nuclear warfare, he now concentrated on the dangers of nuclear power. The story envisions the country entirely owned and operated by business, less concerned with safety than with profit; people are expendable. Radioactive "accidents" and atmospheric pollution kill thousands. Oceanic abuse and dumping of raw waste materials produce new life forms that effectively kill off much of the population, which is too large anyway.

Political and social questions are present in *Los Angeles: A.D. 2017*, while decidedly absent in *The End of the Dream*. In this dimension, *Los Angeles* is a descendant of other negative utopias. Similar to Zamyatin, Orwell, and Huxley, Wylie envisions a citizenry that is powerless and hopeless. The four negative utopias differ, but each depicts strong governmental repression, loss of individuality, and, through a perversion of technology, an unlimited amount of terror. The trilogy of negative utopias is not as despairing as Wylie's, which, with the added dimension of ecological disaster, is one of the darkest visions of the future imaginable.

But *The End of the Dream* is even darker. Ending with the main character, Miles Smythe, alone and weeping because he has "forgotten even the feeling" of hope, this novel projects the final result of man's *hubris*. Wylie had continually warned that Mother Nature would vengefully respond to mankind's harsh treatment, and, since 1968, had been working on a story which prophesized the end of man's arrogant dream of controlling Nature. Unfortunately, he died before its completion. The book was published by Doubleday after Wylie's death, and may or may not reflect accurately the author's final statement. In any case, it does contain the end of Wylie's personal dream of salvaging mankind from himself.

The book is not a novel, but a series of journalistic entries by the main character, Willard Page Gulliver, who recounts the truly horrifying incidents occurring on our doomed planet. There is little, if any, plot structure. Miles Smythe, the brilliant founder of the world-renowned "Foundation for Human Conservancy," has appointed Gulliver to write and edit a record of the events leading to the earth's environmental crisis. Gulliver, both brother-in-law and right-hand-man to Smythe, gives historical, newspaper, and personal accounts of the years 1970 to 2023. The entire book consists of his reports and observations.

The public had refused to heed Wylie's warnings in *The Magic Animal*, where he had cautioned that the price for false beliefs and false assumptions—extinction—would eventually be collected. Progress, he warned, is a relative concept. Along with his technologies, his nuclear power, his apparent belief that he could control nature, has also come man's ability to destroy himself. Yet modern man, writes Wylie, does not believe that any ensuing catastrophes could possibly be the result of the error he calls progress. The "long and ferocious effort men have made to validate their illusions" has succeeded in obscuring any sense of reality at all. The results of human "progress" projected by Wylie in *Dream* are frightening possibilities. His extensive knowledge of science, environmental science, the delicate balance of ecosystems, and biological mutations is apparent throughout the book, adding to its impact.

Gulliver's accounts of natural and man-made disaster are both frightening and occasionally humorous. A dog is blown apart by its own flatulence. Brownsville, Texas, is attacked by killer bees. The bees kill four, but the ensuing panic injures more than five thousand. Drawing on his earlier civil defense position, Wylie presents several situations of public panic to show that official positions on CD are mistaken. Other incidents include weather inversions that kill thousands, blackouts, mutated algae gone haywire, new viruses, and other disasters.

The book's point, that man cannot rule and control nature with technology, and that any attempt to do so will ultimately be disastrous, appears about two-thirds through the book. Gulliver, reflecting on America's readiness to fight and defend herself from other nations, and her lack of preparedness on the issue of the perishing planet, writes about the various disasters that have taken place: "And the lesson is elementary. It asserts that you (and I, of course) are the agents of that slaughter. And it states that whatever is to happen to man today, tomorrow, or as long as man endures is the result of what you (and I) do, whether its net is to improve or poison us. The laws of nature are absolute, inviolable and, when disobeyed, unforgiving. If there should be a God, then He made those laws. He would be a fool to permit their violation, let alone condone the act and then shatter His principles in order to salvage a species that imagined it could thrive by lawlessness."

Conclusion

Philip Wylie died on October 25, 1971. *The End of the Dream*, published less than one year later, revealed what appeared to be his loss of hope for mankind's survival. These last years were difficult for Wylie, who was, in many ways, an anachronism. His books no longer raised anyone's eyebrows. They no longer sold very well either. His health was failing him, and so were his words. The legendary prolific iconoclast was an old man as the Seventies rounded the corner.

But Wylie's impact on America throughout his years of writing should not be minimized. Although some have criticized him for harping on the same themes for a lifetime, he steadfastly stuck to his ideas, developed them, and continually reapplied them to changing social issues. Even more, he was wholly committed to his beliefs, and thoroughly honest intellectually.

His early work in the Twenties and Thirties caused Americans to question their manners and morals. In his novels, he sought to bring his view of American values to the eyes of the American people, who, more often than not, did not appreciate his intentions. *Finnley Wren*, though scandalous to many, was artistically and philosophically sound. Wylie's excoriations and diatribes in the Forties went even further. *Generation of Vipers* and *An Essay on Morals* actually forced the mirror up to the nose of the reading public.

With the country's movement into the atomic age, Wylie shifted his emphasis from manners and morals to national hysteria, the cold war, and the contingency of life itself. The value questions had really not changed, but the way problems were manifested had. In any event, he was still forcing the public to think critically about what he said. Whether or not they accepted was less important to him than if they thought about it. Throughout the Fifties, Sixties, and up to the Seventies, Wylie pleaded with his countrymen to drop their materialistic concerns and look inward to their instinctual centers. Issues and problems might change, he reasoned, but an awareness of man's spiritual nature would lend itself to the appropriate solution. Without an awareness of the underlying laws of nature, there would be no hope for mankind.

Wylie the writer remained hopeful for most of his career. In *When Worlds Collide*, he destroyed the earth, but allowed for a new beginning on Bronson Beta. In *The Disappearance*, he separated the misguided sexes, but brought them back together four years later. In *Tomorrow!*, he destroyed half of the United States, but saved those who could rebuild and create a better world. In *Triumph*, he destroyed most of the world, but, again, provided the raw materials for a new beginning.

Los Angeles: A.D. 2017 appeared more apocalyptic than the rest, but, with the release of his final work, the hope flickered. In *The End of the Dream* the dream is gone; no one will be saved, or so it appears at the end of the story. Progress and technology have failed humanity. Wylie's own faith in science had been shattered; so, it appears, had his belief in man's capacity to create a world of justice and peace.

Nine years after Philip Wylie's death, the world is still functioning. There have been no collisions with giant asteroids, no atomic or nuclear wars, and no major disappearances. But Skylab has fallen, war is still a continual threat, nuclear reactor accidents have become a reality, and scientists have discovered that our food is killing us. The sexes, too, are still going at it, and, in many ways, are as separate from each other as before, despite women's lib. Superman has had a revival. And although angels have not fallen out of the sky, Wylie's prophetic vision has proven to be frighteningly accurate.

Whether or not Wylie is a prophet is not the real point. Wylie, throughout his life, presented possibilities. In both his realistic and fantastical work, his most relevant advice presents itself clearly: This is your world. You must take responsibility for it. Otherwise, you will lose it. Perhaps the end of Wylie's dream is just the beginning of ours.

SELECTED BIBLIOGRAPHY

1. *Heavy Laden*. Alfred A. Knopf, New York, 1928.
2. *Babes and Sucklings*. Alfred A. Knopf, New York, 1929.
3. *Gladiator*. Alfred A. Knopf, New York, 1930.
4. *The Murderer Invisible*. Farrar & Rinehart, New York, 1931.
5. *Footprint of Cinderella*. Farrar & Rinehart, New York, 1931.
6. *The Savage Gentleman*. Farrar & Rinehart, New York, 1932.
7. *When Worlds Collide*. J. B. Lippincott, Philadelphia, 1933 [with Edwin Balmer]
8. *After Worlds Collide*. J. B. Lippincott, Philadelphia, 1934 [with Edwin Balmer]
9. *Finnley Wren*. Farrar & Rinehart, New York, 1934.
10. *Too Much of Everything*. Farrar & Rinehart, New York, 1936.
11. *An April Afternoon*. Farrar & Rinehart, New York, 1938.
12. *The Other Horseman*. Farrar & Rinehart, New York, 1942.
13. *Generation of Vipers*. Farrar & Rinehart, New York, 1942.
14. *Corpses at Indian Stones*. Farrar & Rinehart, New York, 1943.
15. *Night Unto Night*. Farrar & Rinehart, New York, 1944.
16. *An Essay on Morals*. Farrar & Rinehart, New York, 1947.
17. *Opus 21*. Rinehart & Co., New York, 1949.
18. *The Disappearance*. Rinehart & Co., New York, 1951.
19. *Three to Be Read*. Rinehart & Co., New York, 1951.
20. *Tomorrow!*. Rinehart & Co., New York, 1954.
21. *The Answer*. Rinehart & Co., New York, 1956.
22. *The Innocent Ambassadors*. Rinehart & Co., New York, 1957.
23. *Triumph*. Doublday & Co., Garden City, 1963.
24. *They Both Were Naked*. Doubleday & Co., New York, 1965.
25. *The Magic Animal*. Doubleday & Co., Garden City, 1968.
26. *The Spy Who Spoke Porpoise*. Doubleday & Co., Garden City, 1969.
27. *The Sons and Daughters of Mom*. Doubleday & Co., Garden City, 1971.
28. *Los Angeles: A.D. 2017*. Popular Library, New York, 1971.
29. *The End of the Dream*. Doubleday & Co., Garden City, 1972.

ARTICLES

These articles represent only a sample of Wylie's critical essays. They have been chosen for inclusion here based on their use in this book and on their representation of Wylie's diversity.

"Why Colleges Fail Students," in *Saturday Evening Post*, Dec. 13, 1930, p. 25, 130-133.

"The Russians Have Beards," in *Saturday Evening Post*, Dec. 19, 1931, p. 21, 72-73.

"The Quitter As Hero," in *Harper's*, Oct. 1933, p. 633-636.

"Writing for the Movies," in *Harper's*, Nov. 1933, p. 715-726.

"The Illiteracy of Educators," in *Saturday Review of Literature*, June 3, 1944, p. 12-13.

"Sex and the Censor," in *Nation*, July 8, 1944, p. 39-40.

"Memorandum on Anti-Semitism," in *American Mercury*, Jan. 1945, p. 66-73.

"Deliverance or Doom," in *Collier's*, Sept. 29, 1945, p. 18, 79.

"Safe and Sane," in *Atlantic*, Jan. 1948, p. 90-93.

"The Lerner Marine Laboratory," in *Natural History*, Sept. 1948, p. 312-319.

"What About Dr. Jung?" in *Saturday Review of Literature*, July 30, 1949, p. 6-7, 36.

"How to Admire Writers," in *Atlantic*, May 1950, p. 39-43.

"Liberty and the Ladies," in *American Scholar*, Apr. 1950, p. 171-178.

"A Better Way to Beat the Bomb," in *Atlantic*, Feb. 1951, p. 38-42.

"Medievalism and the MacArthurian Legend," in *Quarterly Journal of Speech*, 1951, p. 473-478.

"Science Has Spoiled My Supper," in *Atlantic*, April 1954, p. 45-47.

"Panic, Psychology, and the Bomb," in *Bulletin of the Atomic Scientists*, Feb. 1954, p. 37-40, 63.

"The Mysterious Doctors of Bimini," in *Saturday Evening Post*, Aug. 7, 1954, p. 32-33.

"Rascals Who Impersonate Me," in *Saturday Evening Post*, Mar. 21, 1959, p. 34, 124-126.

"Teenagers Are the Greatest People," in *Saturday Evening Post*, Sept. 11, 1965, p. 10-11.

"UFO's: The Sense and Nonsense," in *Popular Science*, March 1967, p. 76-79.

"McNamara's Missile Defense: A Multi Billion-Dollar Fiasco?" in *Popular Science*, Jan. 1968, p. 59-62, 182.

"Who Killed Mankind?" in *Today's Health*, Oct. 1970, p. 21-25.

SECONDARY SOURCES

Breit, Harvey. "Talk with Philip Wylie," in *New York Times Book Review*, July 3, 1959, p. 9.

Keefer, Truman F. *Philip Wylie*. Twayne Publishers, Boston, 1978.

Moskowitz, Sam. *Explorers of the Infinite*. World Publishing Co., Cleveland, 1960.

Nichols, Lewis. "Talk with Philip Wylie," in *New York Times Book Review*, Feb. 21, 1954, p. 12.

Warfel, Harry. *American Novelists of Today*. American Book Co., New York, 1951.

www.ingramcontent.com/pod-product-compliance
Lightning Source LLC
Chambersburg PA
CBHW022008050726
47499CB00003BA/941